MW00616772

PAUL TERESI

Yes And (ish)

Copyright © 2021 by Paul Teresi

All rights reserved. No part of this publication may be reproduced, stored or transmitted in any form or by any means, electronic, mechanical, photocopying, recording, scanning, or otherwise without written permission from the publisher. It is illegal to copy this book, post it to a website, or distribute it by any other means without permission.

This novel is entirely a work of fiction. The names, characters and incidents portrayed in it are the work of the author's imagination. Any resemblance to actual persons, living or dead, events or localities is entirely coincidental.

First edition

ISBN: 978-1-7372667-1-6

Cover art by YourDreamSeller
Editing by Mandie Gossage & Lydia Redwine

This book was professionally typeset on Reedsy.
Find out more at reedsy.com

This book is dedicated with love and eternal gratitude to Christina, my wife, and my best friend. Also, to my daughter, Samantha. Never give up on your dreams, sweetheart.

Always say Yes And...

Contents

The Clown

A sad clown sat by himself in a hospital waiting room. In one hand, he held a broken rose, and in the other was his novelty handkerchief. They came together for a prayer, even though he assumed it would land on deaf ears. His makeup was smeared by his multicolored fingertips wiping away his own tears. His rubber nose was about to slip off.

In walked an independent ten-year-old girl who had just helped herself to a cup of disgusting coffee. She sat across from the clown. She was not afraid of him and tried to think of something to say. She had not yet learned the privilege of awkward silence others value in times like this.

"I thought clowns aren't supposed to cry," she said indifferently.

"I thought kids weren't supposed to talk to strangers," the clown replied, not meaning to come across as irritable. The silence after his comment quickly became too deafening for even him to sit through. With the raise of an eyebrow, he put his handkerchief away and pulled out a deck of cards from his sleeve. "Would you like to see a magic trick?" he asked.

Surprisingly, the girl shook her head and said, "It's okay. You can take the night off."

She made him smile slightly, and it was the most humbling medicine a pained clown could ask for.

1

"I like your nose," she commented.

"Which one?" He gestured to his real nose and then to the red one as he slipped it off. They both shared a laugh. That's when the doctor came in.

The clown quickly rose and met him at the waiting room door. The doctor put both his hands on the clown's shoulders and informed him that his wife was dead. After the doctor left, the clown stood in place. In one hand was the dying rose, in the other hand, his rubber nose.

"Bad news?" the girl asked innocently, unaware that the clown was in shock.

He looked back at her and was unsure of how to respond. He was a humble man behind that ruined makeup. He approached her and chose his words carefully. He said, "Have you ever had a friendship that wasn't meant to last, but it still managed to find forever?"

She didn't know how to respond. She sat there apologizing with her confused eyes. He walked over to her and handed her the rose. He then put the rubber nose on her nose and tapped it.

He told her, "Don't ever lose it. It's magic." He grabbed his coat and left.

There she sat, now all alone. A dying rose in one hand, and a red nose on her face. It took her the longest time to figure out what he had meant. If a friendship is not meant to last, how can it find forever?

One day she would meet a man who would teach her just that.

Lee

At a backyard bonfire, somewhere in Chicago suburbia, sat a thirty-seven-year-old lost soul. He clung to a nearly empty bottle of wine and the self-pride left over from his lectures to the attending millennial coworkers. This was Lee. However, according to Lee, this was not Lee at all.

Managing a restaurant was how he paid his bills. Being a borderline alcoholic and sex-addicted writer was how he performed his life. It was not a wonderful performance, but he never refused to reprise the role. His constant nostalgia for the innocent hopeless romantic he once was as a kid could never inspire him enough to return to his true form. That part of his soul appeared to have died, and the funeral service was filled with flowers that were meant to be given to girls who couldn't care less. He might as well have been buried alive.

Lee sat at the bonfire, pretending to listen to his co-workers as he drifted in and out of the forgotten dreams he once had. During a Truth or Dare round in which Lee unfortunately chose truth, a woman who used to manage the restaurant with him asked, "Is it true that your plus one for my wedding was a hooker?"

Everyone laughed at Lee as if he should be embarrassed. There seemed to be a judgmental tone in her voice, almost as if she had something to say through that question. Everyone knew they had a history.

3

She continued on regarding that history, "It's okay if you did bring a hooker to my wedding. She looked very professional, if you know what I mean. Not that I'm judging."

To everyone's continued chuckling, Lee gazed up, drunk and stoned, and smiled back. Lee loved history. Class was now in session. "She was not a hooker. She was a friend. Just like you were a friend." Lee slid down in his lawn chair, crossed his legs, and lit up a cigarette. He looked directly at her and continued, "That was a fun day. I got laid three times. Once by her. Once by your mother as we went to pick up the cake. And once by you an hour before you said I do to whatever that guy's name was. All I remember was part of your dress tearing so easily because you bought it at a cheap thrift store, just for a wedding you said you had no faith in to begin with. Not that I'm judging."

Whether it was the uncomfortable silence that followed, or the beer thrown in his face, Lee knew it was time to leave. He called himself an Uber and took a nap the whole ride back to his apartment. By the devil's hour, the girl he insulted at the bonfire sent him a barrage of text messages trying to justify her juxtaposition, only to find herself in a unique juxtaposition underneath his sheets by 6 a.m. once he convinced her to pay for her own Uber back to his place.

As Lee pretended to be asleep next to her, he couldn't help but think about his life, and how the world looked so different in adulthood compared to childhood. In childhood, the world always looked like the beginning of a good movie. Life was a plot filled with laughter. Ego was easy to swallow. A kind thought wasn't so hard. That was then.

Lee barely existed in the present. His soul lived in yesterday. Just because he was buried alive did not mean he didn't dream.

One of Lee's favorite things in life as a child was the smell of freshly cut grass. It always reminded him of those fun summers in the Chicago suburb he grew up in. Every morning he had the same routine. He would rehearse the monologue jokes he had heard on Leno the night

4

before over breakfast, and then try them out on his breathtakingly beautiful neighbor next door. He hoped they would end up like both their parents did, which was sipping overpriced wine outdoors every night and basking in the glow of knowing they got to raise their kids in this beautiful painting of happily ever after.

Lee never had a chance with his neighbor, but when he did make her laugh, it was all he needed to consider his life one of the good ones. They were the same age, but when she grew up and got married at twenty-one, he was still a twelve-year-old sitting in the church pew, debating as to whether God had ever listened to his adolescent prayers.

Lee grew up as a typical 90's child and felt sorry for kids who were born in the 21st century, after war and technology voided the space to dream naively as only his generation could. During difficult days at work, Lee wished he could just travel back in time to when he was in junior high. What a simple life it was. One third of his time was spent playing *Goldeneye* on his N64 console, with the controllers still sticky from all the 7-Eleven summer slurpies he bought with his meager allowance.

Another third of his time was spent on AOL waiting for free porn to download on his dial-up connection, because he did not have the patience to wait for those distorted adult TV channels to deliver the long-awaited, somewhat clear picture of a naked woman. He gave up on those one day when he didn't realize the channel had changed to a movie channel. When the picture became clear, it turned out he had been masturbating to Teenage Mutant Ninja Turtles the whole time. Those mysterious Asian eyes belonged to the Shredder.

The last third went to writing poetry about girls he passed by every day who he never had the guts to introduce himself to, but he knew beyond the shadow of a doubt that he would love them all forever. To pretend he knew what true love felt like was his adolescent drug of choice.

Every Fourth of July, Lee would go to McCarthy Park to watch the fireworks display along with thousands of other local suburbanites. One year, when Lee was fifteen, he saw a beautiful girl smile at him from a distance as the fireworks display concluded. She was with someone, but it did not matter. For those few seconds her eyes whispered over to his, it was if God were looking at him. He tried to make his way over to her through the dense crowd, but he never found her. Just like that, she was gone. Yet, he knew that face would stay with him until the day he died. Indeed, it did. That girl's face would be the last image he saw as his eyes closed to the sounds of the birds singing outside his window.

One night as he stayed home while the rest of his friends were at the Homecoming dance, he pulled out a pen and paper and wrote a story about what he would have said to the girl from the Fourth of July had he caught up to her. The power of his imagination gave him a sense of closure. A sense of comfort. In his head, he was able to kiss her hello, while kissing the memory goodbye. That was the night he decided to become a writer.

His first test came that winter when he asked his neighbor to be his date at their school's holiday dance. He wrote her a note that he felt was the perfect way to tell her how beautiful she was to him. There was no way she could resist. But she did. Easily. When he came up to her and asked if she read the note, she simply nodded her head and explained that she was going to the dance with someone else. This experience broke Lee's confidence. If only the writing had been better, maybe he could have had her, he thought.

The following spring, he rewrote the note into a poem and entered it into the school's poetry contest. He was certain it would place first. It was rejected by the judges, described as weak and unimaginative. Now, Lee was a broken, insecure adolescent writer who was starving to prove himself worthy to a social crowd that couldn't care less. He was not a member of the popular crowd. His voice always felt muted amongst his peers. His heart always ignored by his crushes. If only they could see him from the inside, they would see a soul worth standing next to. Instead, they always just walked on by to someone better. Writing became his escape. It was where rejection came to be numbed, and where hope could learn to fight a good fight for another day.

Lee stayed home from most social events to work on his writing. One way or another, he was going to become the greatest son of a bitchin' writer that ever graced that school with their presence. The more alone he was, the better his writing became. Was it the power of a hungry imagination, or the cold focus of forcing himself to have time upon his hands? He never could give himself a straight answer, but an obsession was born.

By the end of his senior year, he found his proper path as a writer. He knew the best material was found in the moments he felt the most miserable. He was cast to write in a student sketch production and found his niche by exploiting his own embarrassing memories.

His first sketch he wrote was about his first kiss. That memory took place when he was in third grade. His crush had stayed after school to teach him how to tell the difference between drawing the letter b and the letter d. It was some baseball metaphor about how the ball before the bat was the letter b, and the ball passing the bat was the letter d. He remembered being convinced, at eight years old, that this other eight-year-old would be his soulmate for life. They would grow old together teaching their kids about b's and d's using the baseball metaphor that brought their love together. Equally hilarious to the naive thought was her reaction when he kissed her. It was a moment filled with pushing and screaming—calling him a "dick" and a "bastard." Both of which he could now spell out accurately.

His second sketch was about the time he took a cute girl from school to a Blink-182 concert. They sat on the lawn of an outdoor concert venue. It was Lee's first make-out experience. He tried to cover his erection with the picnic blanket, but it kept sliding off. He thought that between the finale and the encore, there would be plenty of time to bring himself down. Blink-182 did not come out for an encore that night. When Lee stood up and tried to walk it off, one would think a missile parade from the old USSR was passing by.

Lee did grow up to be a successful writer. Just not a successful person. As an adult, he still fixated on the feeling of rejection from when his neighbor turned him down. He always felt that if he didn't write well enough, that feeling would come back at a moment's notice. That pain was the last thing he ever wanted to feel again, and he would let so many girls slip away because of that fear.

Lee's first girlfriend in college seemed promising, but she left after telling him she wanted someone who was not a professional blower of smoke up one's ass. She didn't want perfectionist poetry, well-worded excuses, or Lee's favorite, the inspirational apology. By then, that was Lee's only response to someone else being unhappy. He always thought he could write it off, and then get back to focusing on his imagination.

There was one girl that managed not to slip away, although she wished she had. They were both writers. It should have been perfect. The only difference was she knew how to put the pen down, and Lee did not. If only she had met him earlier, younger, before he cared only about the world that lived within his own eyes, they would have grown old together. If only she'd been there when he was rejected by his neighbor and a handful of other girls who had no time for second-place guys, she would have changed his life. It wasn't her fault she was late to his story, but he always treated her as such.

Instead, they both wrote off their heartache into spin-off stories. His went nowhere. Hers became a sold screenplay. His soul could not be more drunk on jealousy.

Lee did go on to write and direct a few moderately successful shows at the Second City theatre in Chicago. Every opening night he invited the girls that got away. Every opening night, their reserved seat was empty. Hoping to replace the spot in his heart he felt evicted from, he found himself falling in love with every lead actress from his shows. They never returned the favor because of how hard he pushed them to meet his vision. He treated each one of them as if it were their job to compensate him for any rejection he felt life unjustly served him.

If at any point Lee felt himself missing that one face that managed to stay awhile, he filled the void with the faces of strangers who welcomed him with open legs and nothing more. Lee did not lose his virginity until he was twenty-three. Once he did, all he wanted to do was make up for lost time. The contacts in his phone filled up less and less with friends and became mostly women he met through sex apps. None of them had a heart to share, and neither did he. Many of their names he couldn't even keep straight. He couldn't remember what they looked like shortly after they left, or what topics they used for bullshit conversations. He did always take time to memorize their eyes as they talked about their own aspirations that he couldn't care less about. What he remembered most was the texture of their bodies. What they smelled like. What their exhales sounded like. How their sweat tasted. He knew only what he wanted to know, and nothing more. He didn't care. They didn't mind.

At thirty-seven, after years of writing shows for the Second City, he was now alone and going through a two-year writing slump. Hoping a change of scenery would help, he quit his job at the restaurant and moved into an apartment on Chicago's north side. His ambition now was to write a novel. The day he moved in, he made his way to the roof to get a look at the view. He tried to ignore his own depression with every cigarette he pretended he did not need.

He lit another one up as he walked onto the rooftop area. He had a whole skyline in front him, but he just stared into an emptiness he knew he had gift-wrapped and handed to himself. He no longer believed in his ability to inspire others through his written words. Truthfully, he never really did in the first place, but that was not how he remembered it.

One day, he hoped to find the soul he used to have as a kid. Noble. Selfless. Like the time his neighbor came home crying because her boyfriend broke up with her on Valentine's Day. Lee immediately took the money he was saving for a PlayStation 2 and bought her every available rose he could find. With them, he spelled out on her driveway, "Your smile must go on." She ran out of her house and threw her arms around him. Her embrace melted him. She kissed him on the lips. Though nothing more ever came from it, the moment stood out as the happiest day of his life.

Moments like that were what he was missing. He would give anything to be that kid again. Granted, that kid never got laid, but kindness was worth more to him than instant gratification. Kindness meant something back then. From time to time, it would lead to one hell of a good story.

Now, more than ever, he missed the smell of the fresh cut grass, the laughter from the girl next door, and even the pretty face he never got to speak to on the Fourth of July.

That day on the roof, Lee was not praying for happiness. He didn't need it. He just wanted life to toss him one hell of a good story.

The day Lee met Lilly, the birds were not singing.

Lilly

T he day Lilly met Lee, she was standing on the edge of her apartment rooftop. She was scared to jump, but even more terrified to live. One wouldn't think it, but there was a pretty face underneath that bushel of hair that had not been maintained in quite a while. Her hair truly was a metaphor for her life; it made sense once, but now was just a confusing eyesore. For this once thrill-seeking actress, now turned victim of agoraphobia at thirty-three, the world seemed like it had been sunny only for a few days in her whole life.

She stood at the edge, feeling both terrified and depressed, but mostly taken by the saxophone player on the street below. She couldn't put her finger on what song he was playing; she just knew she'd loved it once.

She watched a tear fall from her face down to her bare feet. She then looked up at the animals and faces she could make out in the clouds above her. That had always been her favorite game from back when she was still shitting in her diapers at six years of age. Her parents didn't try the hardest to say the least.

Her father was an atheist who hated Christmas and prayers. His wife, of course, was a bipolar Christian who didn't believe in compromise but was devout about drinking the blood of Christ every night. She would eventually kill herself and her husband in a car accident. Lilly always wondered if her mom meant to drive them both off a cliff. It did not matter either way. They both regretted their flaws on the way down. Their very last second of life was spent being distracted by the thought of how it all could have been different.

Hours after the accident, Lilly was left with no parents. In a way, nothing had really changed. Emotionally, she still felt indifferent as she stared at her reflection in the hospital waiting room window. The rose in her hand had lost all its petals, but the clown nose did make her smile, even when she was told her parents were dead.

Lilly's foster parents were an orphan's dream come true. They were a very affectionate couple, both fun and honest. They never went to bed angry, and always woke up blessed. They taught Lilly to never be afraid of the world. At twenty-three, Lilly tried so hard to remember that advice when her father was killed in Iraq, and even harder when her mom died of breast cancer shortly after. She cried herself to sleep every night, almost humored by the thought that she really didn't have to fear life if all endings are predictably terrible.

On her twenty-fifth birthday, she spent half her day drinking in two separate cemeteries. She paid visits to both sets of parents. She tried to comprehend the impossible. She cried loudly in the hope that the angels would hear her. By the time evening had arrived, she was drunk behind the wheel and trying to exit the cemetery. At one point, she lost control of the wheel and knocked over an old tombstone.

Nearby, a group of hipsters her age were doing a ghost investigation. One gentleman in the group confronted Lilly, stating she ran over his uncle's tombstone. After she apologized profusely, he informed her with a charming smile that he was joking. He offered her a cigarette, and though she had never smoked a day in her life, there was no hesitation to accept it.

The kind stranger lit her cigarette and said, "You look like you can use a laugh. Let's see if we can find you one." They went for a long walk, and that walk changed the direction of her life.

He worked at an improv theatre in the city. He showed Lilly a new way of looking at the world. She found something new that was terrifying, but this time it was also indescribably fun. It was live comedy.

Her first improv class, she left within five minutes. On day two, she left within 10 minutes. She hated the looks she would receive when she took too long to come up with a line no one liked.

After ditching her third class, she went across the street and bought herself a beer. As she drowned her sorrows, she held in her hand her lucky clown nose. She wished she knew why the luck was not there. A short time after, the teacher walked in and sat next to her.

"You know it's natural, right?" the teacher randomly said as she received her pint.

"What is?" Lilly asked as she looked around to make sure it was her the teacher was talking to.

"To run away. I did on my first class. You know what the secret is? Start with who you know. If the scene calls for you to be an aunt, be—"

"Be your aunt," Lilly jumped in unenthusiastically. "I've been told that before. I have played my teacher from second grade. I tried to portray my mom, who really was the best character in my own life. I have even played my counselor, who saved my life, or at least successfully put it on hiatus. I even played the nice homeless man who apologized as he was robbing me last week, but I can never pull off a successful scene."

"Come back to class tomorrow. This time, I want you to try something different. Instead of pulling a character from people you admire, I want you to pick out the worst assholes that have ever crossed your path. Become them. Justify them. And in any given scene, you're gonna fight for them to have the best day of their life" A moment of silence took over, as Lilly found those words so profound. The teacher followed up with an inquiry, gesturing to the red rubber nose Lilly was holding. "Let me guess. A good luck charm?"

Lilly nodded nonchalantly. "Yep. It was given to me by a clown the night my parents died."

The next day, Lilly came back to class. She stayed the entire time and had the best lines out of all her classmates. She found herself. Just as important, she found her escape. Once she perfected her craft, she owned the spotlight like no one else could.

Her graduation show was a flawless performance, and the audience fell in love with every character she spoon-fed them. Performing improv introduced her to a life and a love she never knew was attainable. In many ways, it was a type of therapy that changed her life.

During this time, she fell so hard for that hipster soulmate that introduced her to it all. If only he did not go on to leave her in the middle of the night to run away with another girl.

The rest of her twenties flew by quicker than the blink of an eye. Year after year, she would impress audiences with her performances. Offstage, she just wanted to be the likeable fool who stumbled into someone beautiful. She tried so hard to find the good in all the men who took advantage of her, but the sex was never what she pretended it was. She continued to search on, and she searched often.

She wanted to keep promiscuous secrets from her friends and her audience acquaintances, but she made the mistake of opening up to her castmates. They, as actors, could never keep secrets; they just knew how to play the part of honorable friends.

This led her to no longer feel comfortable on the stage, or in crowds, or simply with another human being. She felt that everyone knew her secrets. On stage, she no longer felt idolized. She felt judged for all those nights she wanted to fit in. She felt humiliated for inviting so many strangers to fill so many voids that time was supposed to fill but never did. So many careless nights led to too many familiar faces in the audience that seemed to laugh at her before the punchline. The spotlight wasn't warm anymore, it was an endless shiver. Her performances became shaky. Her lines became lost within the thickening fog in her head.

The acceptance she once felt from the audience was the only drug that worked toward silencing the anxiety within. Once she lost that, it was as if she didn't exist. She was like a ghost in a room who couldn't make her presence known even when she tried her hardest.

The only place she now felt comfortable was inside her own shadow, and even that required locks. Her twenties did not end with a bang. It was more of a final suffocation after slowly walking into the deep end of the ocean.

Once she managed to somehow dig herself out of the emotional hole, she came face to face with the day that killed the clown, as she would always call it. She fell in love with her therapist. He became the only person she was comfortable with. He could see right through her, and she fell in love with every minute of it.

Her therapist was not an actor, but he did play his part well. He rehearsed the same way an actor would. He treated people for depression, all the while hiding his own.

After six months of him treating her, Lilly woke up on her thirtieth birthday and decided she was going to ask him out. She bought a rose and made her way to his office to surprise him. She was met by a sobbing secretary who informed her he had hung himself the night before.

In that moment, all Lilly could think about was everything her foster parents had told her. Never fear the world, they said. Find the humor in life, they said. It is so easy, they said. As she tossed her rose in the nearby trash can, she thought back to her first therapy session.

She was a nervous patient trying to describe how she saw her life. She picked the best metaphor she could that day and explained, "You know when you're a kid, and it's Christmas morning, and you know beyond the shadow of a doubt you're getting exactly what you wanted for Christmas underneath the wrapping paper? It's greatest feeling in the world. Now, imagine ripping open the paper to find nothing but an empty box. But, the fun parents fake you out, and you notice the real gift behind the tree, or somewhere else imaginative. Just when you had stopped believing, you're reminded to believe all over again. Except for one thing…" She paused, nibbling on her lips. "In this scenario, I'm not even in the house. The whole time I was just a pointless snowflake melting against the window."

That day she said that to him, she left her therapist speechless and completely numb. He had now returned the favor. She woke up the day after his funeral feeling like a very disappointed child on Christmas morning. How she missed being a pointless snowflake melting against the window.

Over the course of the next year, Lilly left her apartment less and less. For her, the world had used up all its favors, and it had lost the courtesy of second chances. By the time she was done being thirty, she was agoraphobic. She believed that everyone in life was dealt a different hand, but she could never understand why her life was stuck at a blackjack table where the devil seemed to be the only dealer available.

Throughout the next two years, Lilly left her apartment only a handful of times. Whenever she looked out her window, the world looked miserable and cold. She spent many nights flipping through the same photo albums and reminiscing about the same memories. It was memories of backstage shenanigans with friends, brilliant creations of dialogue with unforgettable scene partners, and the feeling of being a genius when she made everyone in the audience cry laughing. It was all so easy. Perhaps, that was why it slipped away so fast.

On her thirty-third birthday, she managed to make it up to her apartment rooftop. She leaned against the edge of the roof with eyes closed, reliving every skipped heartbeat of her life. Either life was going to end that day, or it was to begin again somehow. She could

16

not go another day without some sort of blind leap toward something representing a different type of ever after.

The only thing that could save her was what she once had. A punchline. The laughter from a stranger. The confidence that came from it. Much like Lee, she felt the best part of her soul had gone astray.

The day Lilly met Lee, the birds were not singing.

Denial

All grief in life begins with some form of denial and ends with some kind of acceptance. For Lee, his five stages of grief all began that day on the roof, where he stood in denial of what he was seeing at that very moment.

Lee stood expressionless, staring at a disheveled-looking woman who stood at the edge of the roof. She wore a black sleeveless Tupac shirt with a black and white polka dot dress that just didn't seem to match. It was topped off by a black bandana tied around her neck that made her look more like an old-time bank robber than a fashion model. Her makeup was sloppy, and her hair was a raggedy character of its own. He wondered if he was an asshole for thinking, *If you're gonna kill yourself, wouldn't you at least make your corpse presentable?*

Even more to his annoyance, she was interrupting his self-loathing time. How dare she. Even in a concerning moment like this, Lee cared more about himself. In that moment, he did not think, *How am I going to save her life?* No. Instead, his thought was, *How long is this bullshit going to go on for?* He hesitated to make his presence known as he noticed her shake as if the summer breeze would tip her over. He quietly took a step closer. He noticed a tattoo on her arm that read, "If I look back, I'm lost." He couldn't help but laugh inside his own head, *You're doing a hell of a job looking forward.*

Lilly sensed someone was standing behind her. She slowly turned her head back toward him and asked, "Well...aren't you going to say anything?"

Lee casually took a drag of his cigarette and looked back at her. Indifferent. He then pulled out an extra cigarette and offered it up to her. "Smoke?"

"Those things will kill you," she said as she brushed off the offer.

Lee now glared at her. "And this concerns you?"

He took a deep breath that sounded more like an irritated sigh. Then, for whatever reason at that moment, he flashed back to the advice his first instructor gave him when he began taking classes at the Second City:

When you find yourself lost, having no idea what to say or do next, always remember two words: Yes And. For everything in life, never say no or but; say Yes And...life will figure out the rest. You have no idea what life will do, but I assure you it will be hilarious. If you're wise enough, you'll pay attention to the lesson life is trying to teach you.

As he remembered that advice, Lee felt slightly less agitated. Still annoyed, but calm enough to try and not be the guy who wasn't one for speeches.

"I don't talk to strangers," she said, now trying to brush him off as well.

He took one step forward. He began to talk in between the inhale-exhale of his drag. "You don't have to talk to a stranger. Just listen to one. I know life is hard, but it's hard for everyone. We've all been here before."

"You've been here before?"

"Well, no," he replied as she immediately turned away from his conceding comment. "But that's not the point. The point is... life is everything and anything."

"That doesn't even make sense."

"I'm well aware," Lee said as he stalled to find better words. "Look,

I don't know what life is by anecdotal definition. I just know that it's real. None of us are exempt from that. That doesn't mean you have to give up." He stopped as he noticed her checking her watch. "Did you just check your watch?"

"I'm wondering how long this is going to take."

She looked away from him and back down toward the street. At this moment, Lee noticed a handwritten note down by his foot. He picked it up and began to skim through it. Something within the words she chose to write in this note caught his eye. He knew, as a writer, that she was not going to jump. Most people, when they jump to their deaths, leave a note with their heart on the page, so people can remember what it sounded like. This note seemed to be missing that. When she saw that he was reading it, she immediately scrambled down from the ledge and swiped it away.

He knew how to approach her now. He chose reverse psychology with a hint of earned sarcasm. "This suicide note...this was the best you could do? I'm not buying what you're selling. Your fuck-my-life thesis is pretty weak."

She shoved it back in her pocket and snipped back, "You really know how to talk to people in these situations. What are you, a psychiatrist?"

"Worse. I'm a writer."

After the awkward silence in which neither party decided to leave, Lee folded his cards and began to head toward the door to exit the roof. Lilly, however, suddenly felt panic about being alone. There was an odd adrenaline rush from making conversation with a stranger. It felt almost like the same type of excitement she had when performing improv in front of a crowd of people she didn't know. It was also the first time in many months where a direct conversation was being shared between her and another human being. As frightened as she was of strangers, there was something different about this one.

As Lee reached for the doorknob, Lilly blurted out, "Okay, you're right! I'll admit, I don't know what the hell I'm doing! I shouldn't even be outside!"

Neither of them could think of the next thing to say. Lee pulled out another one of his "rare" cigarettes and lit up.

Lilly commented as the wind passed the smoke to her face, "They're so bad for you."

He saw through her. He pointed the open end of the pack towards her. Almost immediately, she pulled one out from the pack. When he went to offer her a light, she pulled one out of her own pocket. Silence fell again between them. Lee hated awkward silences. He tried desperately to think of something to say as he took the longest exhale of his life.

Right as he smacked his lips to start saying something, she cut him off. "I like awkward silences."

"You must be having the time of your life right now." Lee, being the typical writer, studied her reaction to his punchline. Just a respectable smirk and nothing more.

"How come the door is fully shut? I put a rock there so it would not close. Did you see it when you came up here?" She sounded increasingly anxious.

"Yes, I tripped over said rock and kicked it to the side."

"Shit!" Lilly began pacing in circles as her anxiety went from a four to a ten. "That is not good! That is NOT GOOD! That door locks from the inside!" She began to clutch her chest and struggled to exhale a series of deep breaths. "Oh my God, so I'm trapped!? I'm trapped! I'm really dizzy! I can't breathe! I can't breathe!"

"Alright, calm down! You got a cell phone? I left mine in my apartment, but if you have yours, just call a friend."

"I don't have any friends in the building!"

"Shocking!" Lee screamed right back at her. "Do you have the landlord's number?"

"He's out of town!"

Her shaky hands pulled out her phone and she began to frantically type out a text. "I can text Beth. She lives on my floor. Three doors down. Or at least I think she still does. We haven't really spoken in the past year. Her ex-boyfriend tried to leave her for me, and when I said no, he tried to go back to her. Needless to say, her birthday was ruined."

"Wait. She lives on my floor too. She lives two doors down from me…you're the other neighbor I haven't met yet!?"

She did not appreciate his expression of She did not appreciate his expression of stunned shock. "Relax! I'm not deranged or psychotic!"

"How would you know?"

"I've been tested!"

Lee seamlessly went from one drag of his cigarette to another as she texted. He became dizzy watching her anxiously pace around.

She sighed a breath of relief and said, "Beth says she's on her way." She sat down and continued smoking what was left of her cigarette. The ashes were constantly falling from her shaking fingers. "Can you sit with me? Please?" she asked him very sincerely, which caught him off guard.

Lee sat next to Lilly. He kept his distance but tried not to make it look too obvious. The space between them was a giveaway. The awkward silence calmed her down.

When their smokes were done, Lilly decided to break the silence with a joke. "There's three guys stuck on an island. They've been there for weeks, and they feel as if they are near death. Suddenly, a genie lamp washes up on the shore. A genie comes out and grants the three men one wish each. The first guy says he wants nothing more than to go home. He returns home. The second guy follows up with the same request. He returns home. The third guy says, 'I'm lonely. I wish my friends were here.'"

22

The joke seemed fitting and calmed her down enough to smile at him. He could not even humor her with a grin. Her grin eased into a chuckle, and then into a louder laugh. Lee could tell her laugh was increasing in volume to hide her frantic short breaths and keep her nervous breakdown at bay.

"Get it? You get the joke?" she asked as she slapped him across the arm.

He changed the subject in an effort to move on from her unstable laughter. "So, Beth should be here any second, right?"

"She's coming from Wisconsin." Her laughter resumed.

"Are you laughing because that's a joke?" he asked.

She shook her head and laughed louder as a tear rolled down her cheek. She grabbed his pack of cigarettes and pulled another one out for herself. She then pointed the open end towards him, offering him one of his own. She pulled out her lighter and lit both of their smokes. A long silence followed. Lee tried to think of something to say to break the silence, but then remembered what she said about liking silences. He thought now would be as good a time as any to try and enjoy one himself.

* * *

Two days later, Lee spent the afternoon staring at a blank page on his computer that now appeared to be staring back at him. The staring contest was pleasantly interrupted by a knock on his door that he had been waiting for all afternoon. It was his landlord, Frank Mangelli.

Frank was a character straight out of a hopeless romantic novel, one Lee wished he could write. Frank grew up in the Chicago suburb of Bridgeport. His family and all his neighbors were Italian. He fell in love with his high school sweetheart, Jackie, and they got married on the steps of this old apartment building that they now owned. Now in his fifties, Frank still fancied his outdated suspenders that would occasionally get caught in his eccentric hand gestures. His personality acted like one giant napkin wiping away attention from whatever snacks were left resting on his over-sized mustache.

Lee invited Frank in, and they sat in his living room. Lee had stressed to Frank the night before how important it was that they spoke as soon as possible. Which was why Lee forced himself to overlook the number of crumbs falling from Frank's donut onto his floor. Lee imagined a nearby village of ants celebrating the miracle of delicious raindrops.

"It looks like you're settling in quite nicely," said Frank.

"Yes. About that. I need to move," Lee stated with polite urgency.

"I assume this is about Lilly. You know she's harmless, right? She just lives in her own little world."

"Have you taken a trip to that world? No? I have!"

"My apologies I couldn't be here the other night to open the door to the roof. I was out of town with my wife. We went to where we had our first date. Have you ever been to Santa's Village? It's not actually a village. It's a theme park."

"If we could focus on my misery, that would make me so happy."

Frank obliged. "You were stuck on the rooftop with Lilly for four hours. How bad could it have been?"

Lee handed Frank a bowl of popcorn. "Settle in."

At that moment, there was a knock at the door. Frank got up before Lee did. "That's my wife. She texted me looking for one of the storage keys."

Frank opened the door and greeted Jackie with a kiss. Jackie was a prom queen that had barely aged. Also from the old neighborhood, she spoke with her hands just as much as Frank did. From a distance, they always appeared like two confused mimes acting out two separate scenes.

"Lee, come here. This is my wife, Jackie," Frank introduced her while

24

flipping through his medieval dungeon key ring.

"You okay? You look like you've seen a ghost," Jackie asked as she shook Lee's hand with a stronger grip than his.

"He just met Lilly. He's scared of her." Frank tried not to laugh.

"I'm not scared of her. I just think she's schizophrenic," Lee quickly corrected Frank's accurate assessment.

Jackie grabbed Lee's hand with one hand and gave him reassuring pats with the other. "I promise you she's not schizophrenic."

"How can you be so sure?" Lee asked.

"She showed me her test results," Jackie answered, still giving Lee's hand a reassuring rub.

"Why don't we all have a seat, and you can tell Jackie and I about your encounter with Lilly?" Frank said, as he also needed time to find one key out of a hundred on his key ring.

Frank handed Jackie the popcorn bowl as they settled in for Lee's story. Lee could not sit. Maybe it was the director in him, but he felt as if he needed to stand and visually act out this story.

Lee took a quick sip of water, the same way a singer would right before going on stage, and he began, "So, I'm stuck on the roof, and it's just me and Lilly. She thought it would be fun to play this game she used to do back in her theater days where the actors would warm up by acting out a movie in sixty seconds. Then two minutes. Then a half hour. Then she just acted out a whole entire movie."

"That sounds like fun." Frank shrugged.

"She chose *Schindler's List.*" Lee paused to take another swig of water, gesturing that the best was yet to come. "That was just the four hours on the roof two days ago. As if that is not enough cause for me to relocate, allow me to tell you about yesterday afternoon."

"This popcorn needs more butter." Jackie got up and walked over to the kitchen, where she naturally knew her way around. "Go on, I'm listening."

25

Lee continued on, "Yesterday afternoon she was being really loud, blasting music and making it impossible for me to concentrate on anything relative to living life. I went over there to knock/pound on her door. It was cracked open. I let myself in. The moment I walked in, there was absolute silence. I still cannot believe what I witnessed."

Lee recounted everything to Frank and Jackie:

As I let myself into Lilly's apartment, it suddenly fell deathly silent. I stood frozen, looking into her living room. Her walls were covered in painted canvases. Each wall filled with over a hundred caricature faces, all painted to look like a studio audience. On the coffee table sat a cue card and a fishbowl with a dead goldfish floating at the top. Behind that was a series of more coffee tables painted and connected to form a homemade stage.

Out of nowhere, the silence was shattered by the chorus of Chumbawamba's 'Tubthumping' blasting from a nearby speaker. I stood there in absolute shock as she gracefully entered her living room and greeted all the faces on the canvas. She then stood at the edge of her stage, reacting to the sound of applause that seemed to be coming out of thin air. I backed up into the hallway quickly and quietly, but I couldn't look away from what this insane person was doing right across the hall from me. So, I stood in the hallway with her door cracked open and watched as the sound of laughter would erupt every time she delivered punchlines that were clearly stolen from late night monologues. It took me an investigative minute to figure out that she was cuing the sound effects from her phone in her pocket. At one point, she had to slow down her delivery because she couldn't find her phone charger. I could not get over how unbelievable this was. She was just performing stand-up in front of a bunch of painted faces and a dead goldfish.

Once she was done with the stand-up portion of her show, she

26

moved into the musical portion, where she covered her favorite songs for twenty minutes. She doesn't sing. Doesn't play piano or guitar. She just straight up rocks out on a recorder.

As she wrapped up a song, she queued an applause and added, "Thank you very much. You're a kind audience. That, of course, was 'I Will Always Love You' from the Bodyguard Soundtrack. Circa 1992. Houston, we have a problem. It's that we miss you so much."

At this point I left to go back to my apartment, astonished that I just witnessed someone perform a musical concert for herself on the recorder. I decided to go back, but I made popcorn first. Maybe it was curiosity, maybe it was the third bloody mary finished by 1 p.m., but I had to go back to see what else this mental patient had in store for the rest of her afternoon. When I slipped back over to the unlocked door, she was sitting at her coffee table and pretending to be on the show 'Inside the Actor's Studio.' She played James Lipton, who was interviewing an Elmo doll with a cup of coffee duct-taped to his hand. What really caught me off guard was that he was answering her questions. Only at the end of the interview did I realize she had an old hand-held tape recorder strapped to his back, with pre-recorded answers delivered with a spot-on voice impression.

If this delusional segment wasn't enough, she would occasionally interrupt herself for commercial breaks where she advertised products found around her apartment. This included a five-minute monologue about her tampon.

Once all the commercials, jokes, and singalongs with no one had wrapped up, she made an announcement. "Ladies and gentlemen, you've been a very enduring audience, and I love you all for being here. Before we part for the evening, let us all take a dip in the ocean," she stated as she cued up Billy Ocean's 'Get Out of My

Dreams, Get into My Car.'

She began dancing all over the apartment. This is when everything changed. This is when I truly felt disturbed. It was here when I realized she knew I was there watching her the whole time. She left her door open FOR me to see this. The entire time, she was performing FOR me. How do I know this? She poured out two shots of tequila and then moonwalked one over to me.

Lee sat back down on the couch. He was physically and mentally exhausted from recalling the whole experience.

"What happened next?" Jackie asked, almost insinuating a romantic connection.

"Nothing! I called her a freak show and went home! But shortly after that, I left to go for a walk. I peered through her open door on the way out and I could see her in the kitchen. She had fallen asleep at the table in the middle of making herself a sandwich," Lee said as he got up and grabbed himself a beer.

Frank reached out for the beer, quickly realizing it wasn't for him as he smoothly pulled his hand back. "Well, I'm just really glad you two got to bond."

"That's not the moral of the story! The moral is mentally unstable people live next door, move my ass someplace else!" Lee tried to calm himself down, patting his forehead with his icy beverage.

"Eventually, you'll get used to her shows," said Jackie.

"She does this regularly? How often does this happen?" Lee asked.

Jackie took a split second to visually check with her husband whether she should tell the truth. "Seven days a week, but only for four to six hours a day."

"She does take off holidays and 9/11," Frank added.

"I can't live like this! I'm a writer! I need to concentrate! I can't do that when I have the Von Trapp family of multiple personalities living

28

next door!" Lee exclaimed as he tore the beer cap off and added it to the growing pile on the coffee table. "I mean, seriously, none of this ever bothered you!?"

Frank shook his head and shrugged. "No. She pays her rent on time. Also I have always been one to believe that everyone needs someone in life that has absolutely no intention of ever judging them. That's comfort you can't buy during hard times."

"What about my comfort? Let's not forget I'm a writer!" Lee asked.

"Do you have a real job?" Jackie innocently asked.

Lee had not found one yet, but insisted, "That's not the point!"

Frank, the eternal optimist, just shrugged some more and tapped Lee's knee with his buttery palm. "Let me give you some advice. I tell this to all my tenants. If you want to have a good neighbor, you have to be a good neighbor."

Lee proceeded to both start and finish his beer as Frank trailed on about some anecdote he couldn't care less about. He just wanted out of this apartment; better yet, out of this life. He swallowed his last sip of beer, along with his hope of pretending, like a kid, that there was a magic reset button on this game of life somewhere.

… somewhere…

After Frank and Jackie left his apartment that afternoon, Lee went for a walk. As he made his way toward the stairs, he saw Beth just inside her doorway hanging up a picture. She was always leaving her door open.

She lived at the end of the hall. From her perspective, she was in her early thirties at thirty-seven. She still had the body of a model, wavy blonde hair, and beige skin like she had just stepped out of tanning bed. She was only fooling herself with her recurring "starting over" attitude after a divorce followed by many failed relationships that were all her own fault.

In his short time of living in the building, Lee had already fantasized about her. Whenever Lee left his apartment, he prepared his speech for passing by her door, which was always open like a college dorm room. Though he would love to sleep with her, he hated the idea of any sort of social obligation being a few doors down.

"Hi," she said as Lee passed, without even moving her head in his direction. Always looking for attention, yet she always played hard to get, even with hellos.

"Hey Beth, let me ask you a question. How long have you lived here?" he asked her.

"It'll be two years next month. Why?" she asked, still not turning her head as she straightened the frame.

"What can you tell me about Lilly?" Lee asked.

She grinned at the opportunity to share some gossip. "I've called the cops on her. Psycho girl was trying to be the next David Letterman at like two in the morning. She was blasting music and talking to herself." Beth shut her door and invited herself outside with Lee. "You heading out? I'm heading out too. Let's walk and talk."

"Her door was unlocked the other day, and I peeked inside. She still puts on shows," Lee said, talking to the back of Beth's head as she walked ahead of Lee's normal sluggish pace.

"She's schizo. I would stay away from her if I were you. She used to harass my ex-boyfriend, and then he stopped coming here," she said as she made eye contact for the first time in the conversation. She seemed only to do that when telling someone what they should or shouldn't do. She liked feeling in control.

"Staying away is kind of hard to do. I live next door." He kept trying to keep her eye contact. He wanted to memorize it for later. He lit up a cigarette as they walked outside.

"Ugh. Please don't smoke around me," she said, waving her hand at smoke that the wind wasn't even blowing her way.

Lee immediately put out his cigarette. He acted so obedient towards a girl who barely looked at him long enough for him to remember what color eyes she had. He couldn't tell if they were green or blue.

"Look, you want my advice?" she asked, looking down at him even though he was taller. "Stay away from her. People like that end up on the edge of a roof sooner or later." She began walking away without even giving him a goodbye gesture of any kind.

"For what it's worth, she didn't jump..." he added in a jokingly optimistic tone, almost as if he were defending her. It was really for the sake of making this conversation last a few more seconds.

"She may not have jumped, but she's still dragging you down." She made her point and went on her way.

Lee picked up his cigarette off the ground. Seeing it was still good, he lit it up again. He watched her walk away.

Her eyes were brown.

Anger

L ater that evening, Lee tried to write the opening page to his novel as Lilly blasted what sounded like French music. Lee decided it was time to have an honest talk with her.

He opened his door, took a deep breath to clear his mind, and walked forward the five feet needed to knock on her door.

"Who is it?" she called from the other side.

"It's Lee. Your neighbor. You performed *Schindler's List* for me the other day."

For a moment, there was only silence beyond the door. Finally, there was the sound of her door unlocking, followed by her footsteps pacing away from the door.

"You may enter!" she shouted from her living room.

Lee opened the door and stopped in shock at what he saw. New painting paper had covered her whole living room, and the scene of a studio audience was replaced by a freshly painted French cafe balcony overlooking the Eiffel Tower. All the walls in her living room were covered in this scenery. Even the painted stars on the ceiling were a work of art. He wondered how she had time to do this. If he squinted slightly, he couldn't tell the difference between standing in France and in her living room.

Lilly sat on her stage at a table for two covered in white cloth. There was a bottle of wine, two glasses, and a fruit basket sitting on top. A soundtrack befitting a French cafe played in the background. She wore a French hat and a white lace embroidered dress from an older period. Lee thought she looked like a 1940's French woman who was taking her last sip of wine to the sound of the Germans marching through.

After taking everything in, he finally got his words to catch up with his dropped jaw. "I wanted to take this time to talk to you, and to be honest about a few things, since we are going to be neighbors for the time being."

"Would you like a drink? I ordered this delicious Cabernet. They also have cream soda." She helped herself to an apple. The crunch of her biting into it was deafening. She took a bite every time he tried to start a sentence.

"If you could keep it down during the day, it would be much appreciated. As I told you when we were stuck on the rooftop, I'm a writer." The pride in his voice was very evident, as well as the implied condescension toward her. "You've probably never heard of it, but I've written for the Second City."

"You write for the Mainstage or Training Center?" she asked, bringing him back down to earth quite nicely.

"That's not the point. The point is that as a writer, I need to be able to concentrate. That is really hard to do with whatever the hell it is you got going on here every day. For example, when I came home from grocery shopping earlier, I wanted to sit down and work on my novel, but you were blasting some song on repeat for over an hour. Was that really necessary?"

"The song you're referring to is 'You Were Always on My Mind' covered by Elvis Presley. My goldfish, Larry, passed away. It happened sometime between midnight and a week ago. That song felt like the perfect one to play as I cremated him on my stove."

"That's why it smells like burnt calamari in here," Lee whispered to himself.

Lilly looked at Lee with an excited stare as she swirled the wine in her glass. It was a long stare that Lee just had to interrupt.

"Why are you smiling at me like a psychopath?"

"I know someone who's looking for a writer!"

"Who? You? You don't need a writer. You need a life."

She quickly cued the sound of an audience reacting to an offensive punchline.

"Would you shut them up!? I'm trying to talk to you!" Lee put his phone down to swipe at hers, but she was too quick for him.

"Why can't you write for me? I guarantee you I am better than any of those actresses you would normally write for. Besides, I gave you like a four-hour-long audition the other day on the roof when we were trying to kill time. You think it's easy reenacting *Schindler's List*? Nein! However, I pushed myself and what did you see? Talent. Skill. Ability."

"I saw a sad, pathetic individual."

"You can't relate to that?" she asked, too honestly.

She had gone too far, and she didn't even realize it until the look on his face changed during the two-second stare-off that felt like an hour. He decided to bite his tongue. He turned around and slammed the door on his way out.

Lilly smiled at the cell phone he had accidentally left on her table. She smiled even wider when she realized it wasn't locked. She opened his phone and quickly took down his number.

Lee suddenly reentered the apartment, having realized he forgot his phone. He swiped it off the table without making eye contact with her and headed back toward the door.

She raised her glass to him as he exited. "Ciao!"

"That's Italian," he said, not looking back as he slammed the door behind him again.

* * *

Later that night, a story unfolded that would be told for years to come. It had begun with Lee making a little progress on his writing. He was writing a scene where two people argued, and even used Lilly's quote to him about relating to pathetic individuals. It was too good not to use. Lee hated to admit that, even within the confines of his own head.

When the hour hit midnight, Lee's phone had received a call from an unknown number.

When he answered, the voice on the other end sounded very suspicious and disguised. Of course, it was Lilly trying to make chit-chat as a poorly impersonated Arnold Schwarzenegger. Lee hung up.

Before he could comprehend what had just happened, his phone lit up again with the same number. Again, on the other line was the sound of Lilly cracking herself up. This time she was doing Al Pacino. Her Pacino was not bad at all. If Lee weren't so busy googling how to block a number, he would have been impressed by how committed she was to the part. Finally, Lee hung up and blocked the number.

A few minutes went by, and Lee was ready to get back into his scene. Suddenly, there was a call coming in from a different number. When Lee picked up, it was Lilly yet again. This time, she spoke with the distinguishable voice-changer from the film *Scream*.

Lee hung up, but the calls kept coming in from different numbers. He had no idea how she was doing it. By the time the 2 a.m. call came in, Lee had had enough. He opened his door, took a deep breath, and walked the five feet needed towards her cracked open door. He kicked it open.

Lilly sat at her kitchen table, trying not to look startled. She subtly hid a list of crossed-out celebrity names under her bowl of soup.

Lee stood there breathing heavily, his angry adrenaline just jogging in place, as he waited for her to say something.

"I don't have an audience sound effect for that entrance," Lilly said, with a deep swallow and the flash of a smirk.

"It's 2 a.m., and I have Barack Obama calling me!"

"Is he okay?"

"I know it's you! You may not realize this, but our walls are paper thin! I can hear you rehearsing your characters as you're dialing my digits! Why are you doing this to me!?"

"It was the only way I felt I could get your attention. What else was I to do?"

"Try knocking! My door doesn't even have a peephole, so already you have the advantage!"

Lee sat down at the table across from Lilly. She casually pulled the knife on the table away from him.

Lee leaned in close to her face to ensure his words were a straight shot. "I'm only going to tell you this once. I don't know what your deal is, but it sure as hell ain't gonna be my problem. You got issues? You go get your shit fixed like a normal fucking person!"

She leaned in as well, oddly enough with a smile, and said, "I can't."

"What do you mean you can't?" he asked, thrown off by her calm tone in response to his raised voice.

"You know what agoraphobia is?" She answered her own question before he did. "You don't. Even if you did, you wouldn't understand. I am stuck here, Lee. The only fresh air I've gotten in the past three months was from the other day when I was on the roof making you laugh."

"I have yet to laugh."

"I know you're just saying that to keep me humble." Lilly got up from the table and walked over to her homemade stage. She continued on, "To perform for anyone is the greatest honor. For me, fate chose you. This whole situation reminds me of what my first psychiatrist told me right before the restraining order. He gave me the soundest advice. He said *go see someone else.*"

"I don't have time for this! I have a life!"

36

"No, you don't! That's how I know you have time for this! Listen, you went to Second City, right? Isn't that where they teach you *Yes And*? When someone tosses you an idea, you never say no. You always say *Yes And*. … Anything past that, you just let life fill in the blanks. And also…per Wikipedia…" She then pulled out an index card with some notes written on it from her back pocket and continued, "Harold Ramis, who was a graduate of Second City, always suggested to writers that they find the most talented person in a room and stand next to them." She then gestured to herself.

"…Is there anyone else who lives here?" Lee asked.

Lilly laughed out loud. "See! I set you up perfectly for a good line, and you didn't disappoint. I think you and I were destined for this moment. Look, when it comes to the art of pretending to be someone else, you and I may not have played in the same ballpark, but we both know the game pretty well."

Lilly continued on about art and life being the same thing. She talked a mile a minute as she sat down at her makeup table, which she had set up on the side of the stage, almost hidden behind her homemade curtain.

The moment gave Lee pause. It took him back to when he would help his actresses prep backstage. He would watch as they applied their makeup so carefully, like an artist filling in the blank spots on an already full canvas. He was always impressed by the way they could perfectly run their lipstick over their lips as they recited their lines at a hurried pace. He missed that adrenaline rush that led up to the curtain rising. The nostalgic excitement of those moments began to overtake his mind. He always took joy in the challenge of pushing an actress to her limits to meet his ridiculous standards of performance.

Suddenly, she stopped doing her makeup and turned to him as if to deliver the most important line of a show. She said, "Lee, don't you see we want the same things? You would love to see me out of this apartment. So would I. If I can get my confidence back as a performer… if I can make strangers laugh with ease like I use to… maybe I wouldn't be so scared to get back out there."

"Are you talking as an actress, or as a person just trying to leave the building and not fuck up at life?"

"Both require a spectacular performance. I really think my first steps begin here. In the process of helping me, you would get your confidence back as a writer."

Lee was trying to hide that he was a bit intrigued. "I feel pretty confident as a writer."

"Admit it…" She smiled when she knew she was spot on. "You haven't been listening to me for the past two minutes. You've been stuck in a scene inside your head that you've been trying to write this whole evening. In fact, even the two characters you're visualizing in your head are starting to show fatigue. You're taking too damn long to add to already pointless dialogue that will eventually be cut anyway because it has no bearing on the overly complicated plot you're also editing in your head at the same time as I'm still talking. Am I right? I'm right, aren't I?"

Lee knew she was right. He did need a break from his novel that didn't even have a title or a purpose. Lilly went back to finishing the touches on her eyelashes. It was amazing how that face looked less uninviting and more elegant within a matter of minutes.

"What are you getting dressed up for?" Lee asked.

"My dreams," Lilly said, winking back at him through the mirror.

Lee thought back to advice his writing teacher had given him at Second City. He was taught to never say no to a writing challenge, and that writing in unfamiliar places would always find a way to inspire the mind of a writer in need. This challenge, however, was one he was not eager to accept.

"I'll write you one sketch. After that, do you promise to leave me

38

alone?"

"No, but I'm very excited about this reluctant friendship."

"We're not friends," Lee corrected her.

He turned to walk away, but first offered his hand for her to shake in agreement.

She grabbed his hand, kissed it, and called him "Godfather." She tried to say it with a straight face, assuming he would appreciate the movie reference.

He did. He just didn't care for her yet.

Sarah McLachlan

The next day at noon, Lee found himself once again in the middle of Lilly's delusional concept of a living room theatre. Lilly anxiously sat on her stage, hoping Lee's blank sheet of paper would turn into an endless clown car of characters for her to perform.

It stayed blank for the first hour. It was difficult for Lee to write in this new setting. The more bored Lilly got, the more she would get up and reenact her favorite movie scenes. Lee kept count. She reenacted twenty-two movie scenes, mostly in English, before his first migraine even had a chance to settle in.

He was, however, caught off guard at her ability to emotionally switch gears at the drop of a hat. She would bring herself to tears acting out a sad scene from a movie no one had heard of other than her. Did she make it up? With commitment like that, Lee wouldn't mind if she did. Then, with just the blink of an eye and a shrug, she would have Lee laughing silently on the inside as she unknowingly quoted his favorite lines from the comedies of many years ago.

As his writer's block continued, her next movie reenactment began as she flipped a fedora hat onto her head while grabbing an old umbrella. She began to whistle a familiar tune that Lee recognized. It was *Singing in the Rain*.

Lee sat there trying not to look astonished that she knew all the choreography to Gene Kelly's musical number. It almost made him adore her. Of course, for Lee, that would be a pointless gesture. Instead, he grabbed her umbrella, closed it, and tossed it to the side.

"Don't you know it is bad luck to open an umbrella indoors?"

"Lee, you and I are spending the whole afternoon together. Trust me, if bad karma took one look at this living room, it would walk on by because it would assume the devil got here first."

"I see," Lee simply replied as he wanted to change the subject away from yet another line he wished he had come up with. "You learned the entire choreography to that song? How long did that take you?" Lee inquired.

"I don't remember. I was eight. I needed a distraction one afternoon while my parents had sex with their door open," she answered, still performing the routine.

After she finished her musical number, she lay across the stage, exhausted, looking up at Lee with her face upside down from his perspective.

"Nothing yet?" she asked.

"Nothing yet," he replied.

"Are you a shitty writer?"

"No, I'm not a shitty writer. I'm thinking. Brainstorming. I don't just rush into ideas. They have to be fleshed out over time," he explained to her upside-down puzzled face.

"Isn't that what shitty writers say, though? No, really. It's like on their card." She proceeded to roll her gum around her finger and used her smile to playfully push him. "Do you do this when you're on dates? Do you sit there in silence and have the girl wait until you're ready to speak a genius line of dialogue that's been fleshed out over time?"

"Sometimes. A lot of writers are like that. We tend to always pretend we're in the middle of a movie. All the world's a stage, after all. We are all merely players. You. Me. Even the guy that's going to dig our

41

graves someday."

She just nodded as she stared at him with an unspoken thought.

"I see you agree with me," he said.

"No, I was just thinking, wow, and I thought *I* was fucked up." Lilly laughed to herself as she got up to glance out the window down to the street below. Even with the window closed, she could hear a cat meowing in the alley below. She and the cat made eye contact, and she smiled at the irony. How the cat longed to be indoors, and how Lilly wanted just the opposite.

"Let me guess, lost puppy?" Lee asked.

"It was a cat," she clarified. "The sad type. The ones you see on the Sarah McLachlan commercials. You know the type? They play her sad song and show the sad faces in the hopes you'll take them home."

Lee instinctively wanted to remark, *I wonder if that would work with pathetic single people.* Instead, he clicked his pen and wrote the sketch he had spent hours looking for. Lilly could tell he had thought of something clever and was pleasantly surprised at how he looked like a completely different human being when writing out a good idea. Only five minutes passed before Lee had completed the sketch. He proudly ripped it out of his notebook, folded it like an airplane, and, like a giddy child, sent it on its way to her.

The paper plane landed at Lilly's feet. She picked it up and glanced through it. "So, what now?"

Lee, shockingly, showed her what his half-smile looked like, and said, "Take it from the top."

Over the course of the next hour, they rehearsed the scene repeatedly. Lilly was like a child who had rediscovered her favorite ride at an amusement park with no lines to wait in. Once Lilly had everything memorized, she was ready for the next step.

Lee went back to his apartment and came back with his video camera. He faced it toward Lilly's stage.

"A camera?" she asked.

"I'm setting you up with a YouTube channel. Thought it would be something you would have fun with. Most importantly, it'll keep you occupied," Lee said as he adjusted her fade light switch.

She helped him set up the stage, but then hesitated and said, "I don't know if I'm ready to be recorded. We never discussed that."

To this he replied, "These takes are between you and me only. You upload only if you like what you see. Trust me, watching yourself is the best way to learn and perfect your delivery."

It was time to record the sketch. The button was red on his camera. The film was rolling. Lee sat in a chair, center stage all by himself. He whispered to Lilly, who was anxiously awaiting behind the curtain with her finger on the light switch, "Lights up. Scene."

```
The Sarah McLachlan Sketch
A man sits in a chair, wrapping up his dating video as he
continues to talk directly into a camera.

LEE
And that's me in a nutshell. So, ladies, if you're looking
for love in all the wrong places, try looking at the right
place. Which is right here. (sheepish reply to himself) This
will never work. I'm gonna need a miracle if I'm ever going
to get laid.

Just then Sarah McLachlan (played by Lilly) enters to the
song 'In the Arms of an Angel.'

LILLY
Sad. Desperate. Lonely. Not knowing what it is like to be
loved. These words perfectly describe this man sitting right
here in front of me.

LEE
```

Wait, what the hell?

LILLY
Hi. I'm Sarah McLachlan. Think about this for a fact. For just $4.99, you can share a meal with this broken man at any fast food restaurant. There's an old saying that when God closes a door, he opens a window. Yeah, he didn't do that for this guy. So please, act now, or he will probably die at home. Alone.

LEE
Again, I'm not feeling comfortable with this.

LILLY
Shut up and face the camera. (Lilly slaps Lee in the head from behind) Call now and receive a discount on a wine and painting class.

LEE
Do I get to come?

LILLY
Shh. No begging. (Lilly pulls out a water bottle and sprays Lee in the face with it.)

"Cut!" he said as he jumped up and turned off the camera. Lee, true to form, swallowed all his pleasantries and played the critic. "The timing of the entrance was pretty good. I thought you could have cut me off and come on sooner, but it still worked. Be careful too when you improvise, because that could have thrown me off. Fortunately, I've had some training with improv, so I was able to center the scene back to the words I wrote. Overall, not bad."

"Do you want to shoot another take?" she asked, with her adrenaline on high.

"Yep. I always do three takes at a minimum," Lee insisted.

44

Lee should have let the camera roll. Instead, he stopped recording to make an adjustment to the tripod and never hit record again. Three takes of the scene came and went. The last one was perfect in Lee's eyes, and he couldn't wait to see it. He jumped up from his chair and ran over to the camera to review it. When he noticed the camera was not recording, he lost it.

"Fuck! God damn stupid piece of shit camera! The button's got to be so fucking sensitive! Of course! Nothing we did recorded! The whole fucking afternoon might as well have been for nothing!"

"We could always just do another take," she suggested, both optimistic and a little scared of his temper.

"What's the point!? I'm not even in the fucking mood anymore!" Lee looked as if he were about to smash his camera.

For whatever reason, in this moment, Lilly thought about the night the clown gave her his red rubber nose. She pulled it out of a nearby drawer and put it on. She sat next to Lee, who looked up and gave her a double take.

"What the hell are you doing?" he asked.

She replied without missing a beat, "Trying to pull your head out of your ass."

Lee just shrugged her off and continued to fiddle with his camera. Lilly swiftly grabbed the camera from him to get his attention.

Before he could even yell at her, she leaned in and said, "Touch my nose and you'll get your camera back!"

Lee felt quite annoyed with the proposition. "What!? What the hell are you talking about!? Why would I want to touch your nose?"

"Because it's magic," Lilly stated with the utmost confidence.

Lee wondered why she said that with so much sincerity. He nodded. Not to humor her, but because he was desperate to have his camera and go back to being miserable. He released a deep, irked sigh and tapped his finger on her red rubber nose. At the very moment his finger touched it, Lilly screamed at the top of her lungs. Lee jumped back two feet. His soul, however, was still jogging down the block.

Lee looked at her like he wanted to strangle her. Unfazed by Lee's death stare, she was laughing hysterically and even snorting at the same time. It was a very infectious laugh, so much so that even Lee relented his stare to the point where for a split second he smirked.

"I caught that!" she said, pointing at the fading smirk still on his face. Lilly leaned toward him, studying his face in pleased fascination. She saw something new in his eyes. In them she saw someone who wasn't always so damn serious. It was like looking at a different person. She smiled back at him and causally introduced herself, "Hi there. I can tell you're new here. I'm Lilly. What's your name?"

Lee didn't want to play cute with her. He stood up and reattached the camera to the tripod. "Let's do one more take."

They did one more take, and it was more perfect than anything they'd shot before. A few minutes later, Lilly had her first video uploaded on her channel. It included an introduction where Lilly explained to any potential viewers who she was, what her situation was, and how this sketch was her first sketch in years.

After Lee left, Lilly lit up a cigarette she had stolen out of Lee's pack and lay on the stage, grinning ear to ear. After her cigarette, she took a nap on the stage and dreamed pleasant dreams of where her life used to be. The stages in her dreams had all collected enough dust to practice her signature on them.

In this dream, she grabbed a broom and cleaned up the stages while singing Bob Dylan's "The Times They Are a-Changing."

A Dance in The Rain

An hour later, she woke up from her nap with a crazy idea. She wanted to go outside. This time she wasn't thinking about the roof. Instead, she wanted to walk out the front door of the building. Perhaps she was still dreaming, she thought, but more than likely it was the uplifting adrenaline that was still left over from her video shoot with Lee.

She looked out her window and saw rain clouds in the far distance. She felt that she could make it once around the block and back before they arrived. To be safe, she was going to bring her umbrella, but there was just one issue. Lee had inadvertently broken it when he tossed it to the side earlier. Lilly decided it was not a big deal.

She would be so proud of herself if she could pull it off. It seemed like an easy enough task. It had been three months since she had exited the building through the front door.

She opened her door and was tempted to knock on Lee's door to invite him, but she didn't want to overstay her welcome with him. She took two deep breaths and began walking down the hallway. Her heart rate sped up and her mind threw up red flags, but she just leaned her head forward and continued. She sped up as she passed Beth's door, but Beth saw her pass.

"What are you up to, Lilly?" Beth attempted to sound like a casual neighbor as she called out to Lilly in front of the friends she had over.

"Just going for a walk." Lilly tried to sound both casual and convincing. She hated that feeling of being judged by strangers.

"Hope it works out for you. It's supposed to storm soon. Might be really bad." Beth spoke in an odd tone. She then grabbed a nearby umbrella. "Here. Take this. Just in case."

Before Lilly could say anything, Beth shut her door. As Lilly began to walk away, feeling uncomfortable with the conversation that had already passed, she could hear Beth say to her friend from beyond the door, "I know it's your umbrella. Relax. She ain't going outside. In fact, I guarantee you she'll be knocking on my door in less than two minutes. Set a timer on your phone."

Those words cut like a blade into her. For Lilly, a punch in the gut would be less painful than having someone bluntly state how much they didn't believe in her. Still, Lilly didn't want to lose the moment. She was determined. She visualized herself dancing in the rain like Gene Kelly while flicking Beth off from the street.

Lilly made her way to the top of the stairs. When she heard thunder, her chest felt frozen. Her legs went numb. The two minutes began ticking. The sounds of a firetruck blaring its horn past the front doors below her did not help. The echoing sirens made her dizzy. She lost her footing and tripped backwards.

She pulled herself up and began to physically admit defeat. When she returned to Beth's door, she tried to quietly place the umbrella against it and walk past. Lilly had not walked more than three feet away when Beth's door opened all the way.

"Um, excuse me," Beth called out to Lilly like a teacher in homeroom. "You knock on my door and return my umbrella properly to me if I give it to you. Do you understand? Someone could have stolen it."

Lilly just looked down, defeated and humiliated.

"Nod if you understand me, sweetheart." Beth continued talking as condescendingly as she could to Lilly.

48

Lilly nodded, just to be over with it.

"Thank you. You can go home now." Beth returned to her apartment and closed the door. She could be heard from beyond the door talking to her friend, "Two minutes. Told you. Take a miracle for that train to be late."

Lilly dragged her feet back to her apartment door. When she went to pull out her keys, she dropped them on the floor. Her hands shook from a combination of anxiety and anger. She dropped the keys twice more. Now, it was time to cry. She couldn't even make out the right key through the tears blurring her vision, and there were only two keys on her chain.

When she entered her apartment, she closed the door and lay down on her kitchen floor. The sunlight from the evening sky shone through her living room window all the way to the edge of the kitchen. She reached out and touched the sunlight on the floor next to her. She could feel its warmth. The rain was late. She cried herself back into a nap.

This time when she woke up, the sun was gone. She looked out her window at two drunk hipsters walking home in the rain. Splashing and dancing in the rain. This was more like the Gene Kelly routine that she had longed to do herself. She fell in love with the carefree souls that never let go of each other, even when they slipped and fell in the puddles. Lilly was fixated on these two beautiful strangers who seemed to have life on pause. Their only reality existed in the soaked laughter shared between them. Perhaps that was the secret to life, she thought. Maybe reality is just a delusional fear, and naive dreams are the truth.

Lilly felt that adrenaline again. It made her smile. It made her get up at two o'clock in the morning and giggle like she was a drunk person gone mad. She put up a tall and somewhat thin canvas on a wall in her living room. She grabbed a paintbrush and the Ocean Blue paint. She painted almost frantically. She did not want this moment to outrun her. It warmed her on the inside to the point where she felt like her heart was sweating. By 2:30 in the morning, she took a step back and admired her new scenery. It was a sidewalk filled with puddles of water reflecting the city lights. The two hipsters were featured, both jumping in puddles.

Lilly wasn't done. She ran over to her shower and turned the water on. Without even checking the temperature, she leaped into the shower. Clothes on. She closed her eyes and pretended she was with her hipster friends outside whom she'd never met. After a few seconds, she leaped out, drenched. Still smiling ear to ear. She then grabbed a watering can she used for her dead flowers that she pretended were always coming back to life. She filled it with water and sprinted back over the painting. She needed to feel as if she were in it. She needed it to be real. She lifted the watering can up high, and the water poured out like raindrops onto her face. The make-believe rain kissed her cheeks, and she kissed back.

With her eyes closed, she pictured a memory so vivid that it was walking right up to her like an old friend. She could remember being a kid and dancing in the rain. She remembered her foster parents joining her and making it fun. It was one of the rare downpours that was met with bright lingering sunshine. She basked in the glow with her foster parents. Her only friends. She could have lived in those warm raindrops forever. She missed how their presence made her feel so safe. No umbrella was ever needed.

Her memory was interrupted by a knock at the door. Lilly grabbed a nearby blanket and slipped to the ground as she threw it around herself. She opened the door, trying to lower her smile as to appear normal. Not wet and demented.

She opened the door and greeted Frank, "Hi."

"Hi." Frank was used to her antics. He politely smiled back at her and asked, "Is your apartment flooding? There's some water leaking into the hallway from your front door."

* * *

Meanwhile, back in Lee's apartment, he was in bed with someone he had never met before. She too had an app for guilty, no-questions-asked gatherings. There was no cuddling after. She played on her phone. He was glued to his laptop as he watched his rehearsal footage with Lilly. He was so fixated on everything she did. The camera captured the truth about Lilly. She was different, and that hooked any eyes that watched.

The girl asked Lee, "What are you watching?"

"Nothing. I was coaching this girl on acting," Lee replied.

"Sounds like a fun gig. How much did she pay you?"

"Nothing. Well, not nothing. She did treat me to Chinese food, and cream soda that I'm pretty sure was expired," Lee answered, still not taking his eyes off Lilly on his screen.

"I'm impressed. She's pretty funny." She continued to watch as she laid her head on Lee's chest and put her arms around him as well.

"Too close," Lee said as he gestured her back to her side of the bed.

It was off-putting to the girl, but she respected his request and returned to her side of the bed. She continued to watch Lee's screen and laughed out loud at the Sarah McLachlan sketch they had filmed. Even the outtakes were fun to watch. Lilly knew how to make mistakes adorable, especially when she would jokingly blame Lee and look at the camera while doing it.

"You have any new shows going on?" the girl asked, not taking her eyes off the screen now.

"No. My last two show proposals were rejected. Everyone's looking for character-driven bullshit," he replied.

"When you do get something going, there's your next lead actress."

51

Everything paused for Lee when she said that.

In that moment, he immediately thought of his ex. She had sold a screenplay and had an upbeat video blog on YouTube on coaching young writers, which included a following of subscribers that outnumbered all of Lee's show attendance numbers combined. Her craft was in the upper-class level of the stratosphere, and Lee wanted to at least snub her from the door of that level.

He needed to feel vindicated. The novel he wanted to write was going to take too damn long. At the Second City, if he needed an ego fix, he could always write a show, and have it in front of an audience within months. That's the quick payoff he was desperate for.

He visited her blog and read comments from young aspiring writers. He knew how they looked up to her. Being the ego-driven writer he was, he wanted them to look up to him the same way they looked up to her. He had a creative thought. A genius idea. Lee being Lee, he had to get to work that very second.

He turned to the girl. "Would you mind leaving?"

Bargaining

T he next afternoon there was a knock at Lilly's door. It startled Lilly, who had just woken up to it. It was Lee, holding his video camera and tripod in one hand. In his other hand he held what looked to be a pile of scripts.

Lilly cracked the door open and peeked through. "Encore?"

"In a way," Lee said as Lilly let him in. He hit record on his camera and attached it to the tripod as Lilly poured herself a glass of wine. "Isn't it a little early for Merlot?" Lee asked.

"In here, it is never too early for Merlot, never too late for coffee, and in between, we smoke if we got 'em," Lilly explained as she pulled one from his pack. She noticed the red light staring back at her and asked, "Are you recording me right now?"

"I have a question for you. What if we made your life a documentary?" Lee asked back. He didn't even give her a second to answer. He went right into pitch mode. "Picture this: we film and document your comeback to the stage. Not the one in your living room, but a real stage. We'll make sketch videos and post them on your YouTube channel. All the while, we'll also document your progress with returning to the real world as well. We'll constantly let the camera roll and record everything. We'll show people the real you, both in character and off book. In the end, you will have your confidence back, and you will have the biggest audience you ever dreamed of to go show it off to."

Lilly felt the pressure building in her chest. She felt like a five-year-old who was about to sing the national anthem at the Superbowl. "When are you thinking about starting this?"

"Right now. We're shooting the introduction as we speak." Lee helped himself to a glass of wine and raised it to her. "And don't worry if you have a breakdown. Breakdowns are good. Empathy is the key to selling you as a likable person despite your mental condition."

Lilly did not raise her glass. She suddenly felt her faith had been abused. Her breathing became heavier, and her heart rate kicked up as if someone had just casually opened a window on an airplane.

Lee noticed and whispered, "If you're going to cry, can I adjust the lighting first?"

She took her wine glass, already spilling from her shaky hands, and jerked her glass at him. The wine sprayed Lee, who wasn't as angry as Lilly had anticipated, mainly because she had missed the camera lens.

Both stared at one another, not knowing what the next move was. Lee kept calm. He knew if he wrote for her, and this documentary became viral, her odd life was his golden ticket. The only problem was who exactly was Willy Wonka going to be in this scenario? Who was going to be Charlie? Both Lee and Lilly couldn't help but be a little curious.

Lilly felt fear, but also felt a need to sound brave as the red dot from the camera continued to stare back at her. She broke the silence by tossing Lee a nearby towel to wipe off what was left of the wine dripping down his cheeks. "I'm not saying no…"

"I'd hate to see what no looks like." Lee zoomed out just enough for him to squeeze into frame as he walked around to the front of the camera. "You said you wanted to get out of here. Did you actually mean it? Or were you just looking for company?"

"Maybe both." Lilly choked a bit on her irony. She had said she wanted someone to write for her, with the hopes of it leading to a return to her old life. But not like this. Not with the world staring. Judging mistakes. Judging everything.

Lee, as if he had read her mind, spoke like a kind character he knew only from his own stories, not from his own heart. "We're in this together. If you have a bad day, I'm sharing it with you. If you get better, but you still can't go outside, we'll stay in and I'll watch the world from a window. If you decide to step out there, and it's terrifying and overwhelming, just remember you're not alone this time. Sometimes it's scary for me too."

"That's the writer talking," she said, brushing his words aside.

"No. It's a friend." The words slipped out of Lee's mouth before the editing staff in his head got a chance to read over the line. He did not want her as a friend. He just wanted her as an attention-getter.

Lilly knew that too. She knew she couldn't trust him. Any sign of kindness was simply a wonderful performance from a self-serving person who, from all outward appearances, appeared to be filled to the core with deceit and selfish motives.

Lee tossed the towel over his shoulder and laid down on the kitchen table the stack of scripts he had been holding.

"What are these?" she asked.

"These are a collection of my scripts that never got performed at the Second City."

"I'm touched that you looked at this gigantic pile of rejection and thought of me," she smirked as she began to flip through them. She then nodded in agreement with Lee's pitch. "Deal. I just have one rule, Lee."

"Lay it on me."

"Don't fall in love with me," she said with a straight poker face.

Lee could not tell if she was being serious or not. The slight movement of her lips trying to hold in a laugh gave her away.

They spent the whole afternoon and into the evening rehearsing character after character, sketch after sketch. They tossed aside the ones that did not work and rewrote the ones that did. Lee felt like a dead man brought to life again as he wrote and directed every blink she took. She too felt like she was worth giving a damn about. It had been so long since she last felt that way. That feeling of someone paying special attention to her left her speechless when she wasn't reciting Lee's lines. The camera recorded the entire day. It captured their evolving chemistry so perfectly.

Finally, it was seven o'clock, and they had been rehearsing characters since noon. Lee packed up his camera and was preparing to exit without giving a proper goodbye. No hug. No "See ya tomorrow." He would just turn the knob and go without ever looking back.

As he went to turn the knob, Lilly desperately blurted out to him, "How about a walk!?"

Lee stood still, trying to study her to figure out if she was serious. She wasn't. She just didn't want him to leave so quickly. She had grown attached to him the same way a child grows attached to their favorite swing set at recess time. She just did not want the moment to end.

"Alright. Let me just go grab a backup battery from my apartment." Lee walked out into the hallway.

Lilly grabbed her keys and came with him. Slowly.

Once they entered his apartment, he sat her on his couch and gestured to her to stay, like she was his new pet from the store. He proceeded to his room to change out of his wine-stained shirt as quickly as he could. Like an untrained pet, Lilly began wandering around his living room. Her wandering led her to recognize a pink photo album leaning against a few self-help books on a shelf. When she went to flip to the first page of the album, Lee immediately appeared behind her and swiped it away.

Lee snapped at her as he put it back on the shelf, "Don't ever go through my shit!"

"Alright! Jesus! Relax! What's the big deal? Are you in the Witness Protection Program?" Lilly playfully asked as she jumped back on his couch, completely unfazed by his frustration with her. She didn't ask it at that moment, but she was dying to know what was in that photo album. And why pink?

He threw on his backup battery and began to record Lilly, who was sitting on his couch with her knees bouncing in nervous excitement.

"So, Lilly, you just wrapped up your first full day of rehearsal. Tell the people watching this what you just told me."

"I'm going for a walk today."

Lee added his commentary from behind the camera. "Lilly and I were talking earlier during rehearsal, and our goal was to get her over to her favorite Greek restaurant, Olympia Fields, by Christmas. It is currently September 24th. I don't know what to say, Lilly. Don't recover too quickly. Ten-minute documentaries are hard to market."

He was teasing, but that comment threw Lilly off. To her, it almost sounded like he was hoping she would fail. She could not shake off that feeling as she got up to walk out the door with him.

He continued asking her questions. "What inspired you to do this?"

Lilly looked down for a moment, trying to think of an honest answer that didn't sound too cliché, but still had an innocent delivery with what sounded like an Audrey Hepburn line, "I miss dancing in the rain."

"There's no rain in the forecast," Lee added.

"I'm aware, you idiot. Edit your part out." Lilly hated when Lee injected reality into her blissful lines.

Lee never shut off the camera; he continued to roll the film as they moved off the couch and into the hallway. Lilly walked slowly and took her time. She looked as if she were walking through a hallway that was five hundred years old and built on buckling stilts. She knew she'd walked better the day before, but the pressure of the red dot from the camera behind her tightened every muscle in her body. She got to the top of the stairs and hesitated to take the first step. She felt the shadows of anxiety sliding their hands over her neck.

Lee never picked up on her growing anxiousness, or the fact her fingers played the same two piano notes on her side. He never noticed her breath getting subtly heavier, or the goosebumps growing rapidly across her arms. Of course, he wouldn't be able to see the butterflies in her stomach chewing away at her insides. Their wings like sharp fluttering icicles, freezing the warmth she was still trying to embrace, which was now turning into a nauseated, frostbitten stomach with an overly dry tongue on top.

She knew she was in over her head, but didn't have it in her to speak up. How dare she disappoint the red light looking at her, she thought. The world now felt like it was splitting open right underneath her knees.

She pushed herself forward and reached the very bottom of the steps, but the dizziness was overwhelming. The sun that reached out through the glass on the front doors was blinding. Once she had reached the doors, she paused and leaned her forehead against them. She peeked through the glass and could see a crowd of people who just so happened to be meeting someone else in the building for a bar crawl. They spoke loudly and offered little space to move within the front patio area. The butterflies in Lilly's stomach were now piercing her skin. The faintness she felt now eclipsed her optimism, and the world felt like it was glaring down at her from a rising height.

Lilly opened the front door, and the slightest breeze was enough to make her fall to her knees. Lee, being Lee, continued to film before a stranger took notice.

"Is she okay!? Why are you filming her!?" the stranger lashed out at Lee.

"Is she having a stroke!?" another shouted.

All eyes were suddenly on Lilly. Now the world was terrifying.

"Hey asshole! Quit filming her!" the first stranger shouted as they shoved Lee.

"She's fine! We're just shooting a film!" Lee shouted back at them. He then whispered to Lilly in an agitated tone, "Alright, can you quit being dramatic? You're freaking people out."

People began to crowd Lilly. She tried to find her voice to push them back. It was gone. She managed to gather enough strength to limp her weak legs back toward the stairs, but collapsed right as she reached them. At this point, Lee finally put the camera down.

"Good idea, we should go back upstairs," he said, smiling back at the confused crowd. It was the standard nervous reaction of the schmuck he was. Instead of worrying about her safety, he was more worried about his appearance to the crowd inching closer through the front door.

Lilly screamed as Lee went to grab her arm, "DON'T! DON'T FUCKING TOUCH ME!"

Lee began to panic as all the eyes on him felt heavier. "Calm down! What do you want me to do!?"

Lilly kept trying to scream back at him. It was painful to hear that crack in her voice. The body wants to scream, but the vocal cords can produce only so much volume. Lee, again being Lee in the moment, thought only about how he wished he had caught that on his camera.

"RELAX! BREATHE!" he shouted at her, trying to get her to calm down.

"SHOUTING DOESN'T HELP! JUST LEAVE ME ALONE!" she shouted back in angry panic once her voice fully returned.

Only Lee would be annoyed with someone having a nervous break-down. He whispered back, initiating a more subtle shouting match, "You're making a God damn scene! Quit acting like a fuckin' crazy person!"

"I'M NOT CRAZY!" she shouted, which seemed to silence the

entire world. She grabbed the railing and pulled herself up the stairs frantically. Very frantically. She tripped multiple times on the first few steps and shouted to the people at the bottom of the stairs looking at her, "STOP STARING!" She raced up the rest of the stairs and was out of sight.

Before following her, Lee turned to the crowd of people staring at him. "I don't know her."

"Why were you recording her?" a voice from the crowd asked.

Lee could not think of any intelligent lie. There were none. He just quickly turned his back and made his way up the stairs.

As Lilly reached her floor, her sobbing was so loud that Beth could not ignore it as she opened her door to see what was going on.

As Lilly ran quickly past her, Beth commented to herself loud enough for Lilly to hear her, "Jesus. Did the groundhog see their shadow?"

She commented to Lee as he passed, "Six more weeks of winter. That's fine with me, we could use a cool down in September."

Lee wasn't sure how to react to that. He looked like he was caught with his pants down. He shrugged his shoulders and shook his head. He might as well have been wearing a shirt that said, 'I'm not with crazy.'

"You two friends now?" Beth asked in a humorous tone.

"She's not my friend." Lee chuckled at her question.

Right when he was about to settle into his chill pose of leaning against the wall to ask how her day was, she interrupted his changing of the subject pose by closing her door. No goodbye. She just gave her two cents to Lee for his obese piggy bank.

Lee walked down the hall to Lilly's door, which was still open. He opened his camera and began recording. She stood in her doorway with her tear-soaked humiliated eyes. She wanted to make sure Lee was in front of her so she could slam the door in his face.

"She's not my friend?" she repeated Lee's words back to him.

"Are we friends?" he asked her.

She slammed the door shut.

Lee sarcastically responded as he closed his camera, "We'll just slide this in the outtakes reel."

Lee went back into his apartment that evening and reviewed the footage of Lilly breaking down. It should have been hard for him to watch, but he was wearing his director's hat. He focused more on the stock he knew people put into documentaries for the pure entertainment of watching someone burn alive. He knew what the raw footage needed. It was added context. He needed Lilly's whole story. The audience would need to know who she once was to understand who she was now fighting to be.

He spent the rest of the night mapping out an organized rehearsal schedule for the both of them. He now knew how to manage expectations. His. Hers. The audience's. Lee had a plan.

Meanwhile, in Lilly's apartment, in the corner of the living room, there was a painting she freshly did of a faceless mother down on one knee, arms open for a hug. Lilly crawled in front of it and cried, pretending she was being embraced. Her face leaned against the mother's arms, the dripping paint now in her hair. She didn't care that she was a mess. She cared only about the warmth from the imaginary embrace.

Later in the night, the hour had reached one o'clock. Lee gave up on trying to sleep. He grabbed his camera off its charger and took a second to make sure he looked decent in the mirror. He walked over to Lilly's door and set up the camera on its tripod. He hit record and knocked. There was no answer, but her lights were on right beyond the door. He knew she was probably just ten feet away.

He leaned his head on the door. "Lilly, it's Lee. Can I come in?"

No answer.

He continued on, "I'm sorry about earlier. I kept recording because people need to see what it's like. They need to see all of you for them to know who exactly it is they are rooting for. Ya know?"

Still no answer.

Lee waited for a moment, and then turned his back on the door. Suddenly there was an answer.

Her voice, still weak and defeated, requested beyond the door, "Tell me a joke."

"You want me to tell you a joke?" he asked to clarify.

"Laughter heals all wounds. I'm hurting. Please. Tell me a joke." Her voice cracked on the last sentence.

Lee was not a funny man. He could write funny when given days or weeks at a time, but not within a moment. He stood there racing through an empty rolodex of humor in his head.

First, he tried a knock-knock joke. Then, he tried a classic approach of someone walking into a bar. After that, he spent ten minutes reading the quickest jokes he could find on his phone from the internet. Finally, she opened the door.

"You finally heard one that made you laugh?" he asked.

"No," she answered.

"Why did you open the door?"

"Even train wrecks get old." She walked away from the door to let him in.

He walked in with his tripod in hand. He quickly set up to record their conversation. A part of her was disgusted that he would even bring it in her apartment after earlier, but her loneliness vetoed the urge to scream at him.

While Lee set up his camera, Lilly sat on a trapeze swing she had set up by her window. She swung on it like a sad child on the playground as she stared out the window. It was another day wasted. She was used to this feeling by now, but this day was supposed to be different.

Lee zoomed in on her as she began to speak about earlier. "I hate the way people look at me. It always makes me feel like I just woke up in a falling elevator."

"Why was the front door scarier than the roof?"

"On the roof, it was different. I was alone. Above everything. Nothing to look down on me but the sun, a few clouds, and a bird that seemed to be holding its breath when looking at me. Life was peaceful. There were no surprises ... till you showed up."

"Peaceful? You were standing on the edge about to jump off with a suicide note off to the side," Lee reminded her.

"I think you and I both know I wasn't going to jump. I just wanted to play the part. Was I convincing?" she asked Lee with honest curiosity.

"If you weren't, I would have just finished my cigarette and left. It wasn't till I read your note that I knew you were full of shit. Truth is always found in the words we choose. Your words alluded to a person who wasn't suicidal. You were just a lost person who was being dramatic." Lee always delivered honest responses with a hard tone.

"You cared enough to stay with me. That has to count for something."

"I didn't have a choice. The door was locked."

Lilly redirected herself slightly to bring up another point. "I think the other reason I freaked out downstairs was you tried to hold my hand at one point. I don't like when people hold my hand. It's just something I have always been weird about."

"I actually wasn't trying to hold your hand, I was trying to grab your arm, but missed because you were acting so frantic. But not to worry, I don't ever foresee a circumstance where I will be holding your hand," Lee joked, but it was with a straight demeanor.

"Was there supposed to be an upside to this conversation?" Lilly chuckled to herself as she continued to stare out the window. "I'm not ready to live my life again. You want to make a documentary on me returning to the stage, but I can't even walk across the street. I remember the last show I did was at this small theatre, where I kept feeling like I was going to fall off the stage as if it were shrinking. There were only forty people in the audience. Now, I can't see myself performing in front of forty people."

"I can't see it either," Lee said in that straightforward tone she hated. "You can't do shit right now. You're not ready. You're not even close."

That tone. That demeaning tone of hard truth. She was waiting impatiently for this so-called writer to plant his optimistic spin on it.

Waiting... Waiting...

Lee had it in his back pocket the whole time. He just preferred to take his dear sweet time with it. He sat down on the edge of the stage and was face to face with her. He pulled out a written rehearsal schedule and handed it to her. It had hours upon hours of rehearsals planned for weeks, along with deadlines to keep pace with.

His optimistic tone wasn't much different than the one he used for truth, but it was good enough to ease Lilly into his speech. He waited until she looked up from the sheet, so he could read her reaction. He could tell there was a sense of trust in what he had written out.

Lee stood on top of her stage and slowly walked around it as he began his speech to her. "You're the worst person in the world to be brilliant. And I am a blind kid trying catch a butterfly. You have so much going against you. You can't memorize lines for shit. You break character more often than you realize. Your choices when improvising destroy any world you try to build. Your characters die at your own feet. If that weren't enough to disregard any burden of hope in yourself, you also have to deal with the fact that if you do steal a miracle from God, and you do pull off the scene of a lifetime, you are still stuck here. With nothing. And no one. You might as well be taking a bow in a coffin."

Lilly looked at Lee with an unwavering glare. Chin up. Her teeth grinding as she continued to wait for her dignity to make a surprise guest appearance.

Waiting... Waiting...

Lee was ready to conclude as he slowly took a seat in front of Lilly and continued, "But what we don't appreciate about a blind kid chasing a butterfly is that he will catch it. He may not see what others see, but he can hear everything. He can hear the heartbeat between the wings. That's all it takes."

When those words finally arrived, she began to embrace them. She took in everything he just said, and the look on her face begged for more.

Lee leaned in closer, and again gestured to his schedule. "You said you can't perform in front of forty. So, start with four. A live performance here in front of four people. This happens in one month. After you cross that bridge, you do a performance here again a month after that. Then, it will be forty. In between everything, we write, we perfect, and we upload. Build your channel. Build your audience. Build your confidence. If you follow me and listen to everything I tell you to do, I swear to a God, who is probably laughing his ass off right now, that you will walk out of here a true actress. The one you always knew you could be."

She looked out the window and took a deep breath. She then turned to Lee with a grin and said, "If you have a cigarette, I'm all yours."

"I decided to quit today," he replied.

"You had to choose today of all the days?" she asked him in a playful tone. She got off her trapeze to sit next to him on the stage. "Who's going to be the four people I perform for?"

"Frank and Jackie are obvious choices. Let's see. Who else? What about Beth down the hall?"

Lilly tilted her head at Lee. "Beth? She hates me. After the incident with her ex she has called the cops on me twice. She has told everyone in the building I have multiple personalities."

"You kind of do," Lee replied.

"Yes, but you've met them. They're all wonderful."

65

"Alright. So no on Beth."

Lilly had a change of heart toward the idea. "She can be here. It'll be a good test to perform knowing there is a critic in the audience."

"I'm a critic."

"No, you're an asshole. There's a difference." Lilly said this straight-faced, but then relented with an innocent laugh. "I like this plan. You're right, we should start small. I'll have Frank, Jackie, Beth, and I'll invite Judy. She's the nice delivery lady that brings me all of my craft store deliveries."

"Does she know your...you know...condition?" Lee asked, trying not to ruin the positive momentum.

"Yes, she's aware. Last Christmas she brought me enough painter's paper to cover a museum. Jackie's really nice too. She knits me sweaters every Easter and Christmas."

Lilly finally felt at ease. A sense of control had returned. Looking ahead, she didn't have to plan for the entire world, or twenty people crammed onto a patio, or any other random equation she didn't have the answer prepared for. She just had to focus on the goal ahead. It would be a live performance. Four people. In one month. This audience would work.

As Lee stood up, Lilly grabbed her trapeze swing and offered it to him.

He shook his head at her gesture to share, and gently pushed the swing back. "No, thanks. I have to pack. I have a three-day orientation session in Wisconsin. I finally found a nine to five tech job that allows me to work from home half the time. Evenings and weekends off," Lee explained. "I'll be back this weekend. We'll begin then."

Lee, not wanting to ruin the moment or say something that would generate second thoughts from her, packed up his camera and left in a hurry. He always did that. He never took the time to properly greet her or say goodbye. He felt the fact he was sharing his life was a kind enough gesture.

She sat down on her swing. Motionless. She stared at the door for a few moments. That turned into a half hour so quickly. She couldn't stand him, and yet one thing she would never admit was how much she missed him whenever he left. He was less than a hundred feet away, but it was too far. She knew it was because she had been isolated for so long, but she didn't want to dismiss the excitement of having someone around. Even if it was Lee. Even if he did sometimes chew on her dignity like it was bubblegum, she would always be willing to hand him another piece if it meant sharing the evening with someone.

* * *

The next morning, Lilly woke up still feeling disappointed about not making it outside the day before. The awkward feelings were still fresh in her stomach. She wanted to knock on Lee's door and beg him to try it again. She couldn't. Lee had left for the day. She knew it was going to be a long three days without him, but she had some ambitious ideas on how to pass the time.

Lilly thought to herself that Lee was right in that she did rush into a challenge she was not prepared for. Perhaps if she practiced getting to the front door, and even go so far as to step foot outside of the apartment building, Lee would be proud of her. For Lilly, that would be a lot. She loved the idea of surprising him. She felt driven by her embarrassment from the day before.

On day one, she got to the end of the hallway, but would retreat and try again when trying to go further. Every time she gained an inch, she felt stronger, but then back to pathetic when someone would come up the stairs with the same type of confused eyes that were glaring at her the day before. By the end of the day, she tried the stairs again, but felt too dizzy after taking just three steps down. She assumed it would be easier with Lee not behind her, but found it was more difficult. Day one ended with her sitting on the top step of the stairs. She pushed her earbuds in as deep as they could go. She took calming breaths as she listened to a playlist she made that was composed of instrumental piano covers. She closed her eyes and visualized what tomorrow might be like.

When day two arrived, there was progress, but she'd get stuck in the middle of the stairway. She would have to sit as the pedestrian noise from the patio garden just outside the front doors would begin to rise to a deafening pitch that only she could hear. Even with her earbuds in, her legs would buckle, and her hands would shake. Whenever someone was behind her, she felt panicked, like someone was after her. When someone began to walk up the stairs, she would panic that she was in their way and sprint back to her floor.

At one point, she ran directly into Beth, who looked fed up with Lilly as she shouted, "You almost knocked me over! What is wrong with you!? Are you blind now too!?" Lilly wouldn't even look back to respond as she fled back into her apartment and slammed the door.

Day three was the day in her mind. Nothing was going to stop her. It was walk to at least the front door or die trying. She had to prove herself worthy to Lee, a man who looked at her like expired milk. She tried to look past that. There was a finish line she had her heart set on crossing.

It was raining. She did not have to set foot outside. She no longer owned an umbrella, and that justification made her feel at ease. If she could just get to the front door and open it to feel one single raindrop, that would be good enough for her. Her mind suddenly had more control in compartmentalizing the fear. It was now like a small Rubik's cube with most of the colors aligned. The ones that weren't, she could just peel off.

She took three deep breaths and opened her door. She walked down to the end of the hall. Then, she made her way to the middle of the winding stairs. As someone passed her, she just looked down, closed her eyes, and attempted to smile politely as the piano covers played on. Onward she made it to the bottom of the stairs. Standing there was Beth, making a sales pitch to three potential customers for her beauty line.

"Can you guys give us a minute?" She pardoned herself away from her customers and gestured to Lilly go back up the stairs. "Can I talk to you?"

Lilly nodded. She hadn't felt like this since she got a detention for cheating on a test she took twenty years ago. A guilty sweat began to form on her forehead by the time they reached the top step.

Beth opened the door to her apartment and walked in. Lilly wasn't comfortable enough to follow. Fortunately, she wasn't invited in. Beth was back after a moment with a gift for Lilly. In Beth's hands was a coloring book for adults. She didn't bother to add crayons, or even take off the $.99 red clearance sticker.

Beth gave her a smile that would make even the devil jealous, assuming he created passive aggressive smiles. "I felt bad about the other day when I yelled at you for bumping into me. I know you have... well, whatever it is, I know it's hard. I now work from home with my beauty line that I promote on my Instagram, and I was thinking, since I'm going to have a lot of people coming in and out all the time—"

Lilly finished her thought, "You want me to stay put and not be in your way."

"That's not it at all!" Beth laughed lightheartedly and continued, "I just know you have to stay in a lot, and I thought this would help make things a little easier. Maybe help the time pass. My grandma lives in a nursing home and she loves these. Us girls have to look out for each other, right?"

Lilly smiled as best she could. She was not a good actress when it came to bullshit. Lilly thanked her and went to make her way back towards the stairs.

Seeing her customers were at the bottom of the steps, Beth took a step forward, trying not to make it obvious that she was cutting off Lilly's path to the stairs. "Why don't you put it in your apartment. I'd hate to see you lose it."

Lilly stood there trying to push herself to say something, but she had neither the patience, nor the courage to stand up for herself. The moment of silence irritated Beth, who was trying to not feel awkward.

"Okay, thank you. You can go home now," Beth said as she made her way back down the stairs.

Lilly lowered her head in defeat and retreated to her apartment. She shut the door and leaned her forehead against the door with all her weight. Her tears made their natural journey to the center of her cheeks before gravity pulled them onto the floor next to her feet. After a few minutes had passed, she wiped away her tears and rubbed them off the floor with her shoe. Again, three deep breaths. Again, she opened the door, determined to win this moment back.

Before her shadow even set one foot outside the door, she could hear laughing down the hallway. She pulled herself back a step and crept one eye down the hall. It was Beth and her clients. All of them were exchanging wide-eyed looks in astonishment at the stories they were hearing. Lilly couldn't hear Beth's voice clearly, but she knew she was talking about her.

Beth was going on and on, dragging out the conversation. After a few minutes, Lilly took a second step back and slammed the door. Beth and her friends could be heard laughing.

Lilly took Beth's gift and tossed it in the garbage can. How badly she wished she had a cigarette. How badly she wished she had Lee. Even though, in that moment, who knew if he would even look in her direction. In that moment, she wouldn't even care as long as he had a drag to share. She was aware of that. She couldn't pretend she wasn't. It sank her even deeper.

* * *

When Lee returned, the next two weeks passed quickly. Every day, at least one special character was found and spared from the others that were tossed out. The struggle Lee had with focusing her mind, which raced like a butterfly, continued to test his patience. But Lee was happy to be in a theatrical realm again. He felt at peace to be on a stage again giving direction. And Lilly was happy to receive it. His smart balance between knowing when to push her and when to let her get lost in her imagination was key to her redevelopment. Within days, he could see vast improvements. Most days were productive and peaceful. Most days...

Some rehearsals resulted in loud arguments as if they had been married for twenty years. Neither would back down, and the jabs would only get sharper as the hours dragged on. Lee was never bothered by this as long as the camera was rolling.

During one such instance, Lilly kept moving out of frame from the camera after Lee had given her specific blocking instructions to avoid that issue. He reached the point of beyond irritated and snapped at her, "You keep going out of frame! Can you not hear me when I repeatedly tell you not to go past this mark!?"

"Maybe it's not me, ya know!? Maybe the scene is not set up properly!"

"The set up is fine! Just stay focused for once in your life! Jesus Christ! Along with agoraphobic, people watching this are going to think you're deaf, blind, and fuckin' retarded!"

Lilly HATED that word. She immediately responded to the insult by whipping a vase against the wall. He could tell she was glancing for something else to throw and changed his tone to be slightly more optimistic. "Your memorization is spot on, though."

She nodded through the angry panting and replied, "Thank you."

And the next take was perfect.

Both had very odd temperaments and varying levels of patience with one another. Seats were pulled out for ego, while humility was checked at the door. Humble moments were few and far between. They did share brief moments of it when it came to editing the sketches they filmed. Lilly was always quick to compliment Lee's writing after the fact. Lee was too busy thinking about how he was going to edit footage of them arguing to make himself look like the lesser fool.

At the end of each day that passed, both could honestly, but silently, appreciate the fact they had done everything they could to make themselves look entertaining if nothing else. On camera and off. In character and as themselves.

By the end of those two weeks, they had a dozen polished sketches ready to be uploaded onto Lilly's site. Lighting was okay after Lee did some research and bought some lighting equipment off a friend. He even helped set up a professional curtain backdrop for her stage. Every sketch had either a simple curtain backdrop or a painted scenic background Lilly provided herself. Everything was pretty much filmed as is. No special effects.

The first new video uploaded from these weeks was a montage of Lilly on her homemade stage nervously reading lines, rehearsing characters, and staring out windows. It was cut like a trailer with Lee narrating about her situation. The coming attraction portrayed a tortured, yet attractively unique soul trapped in her apartment like some urban tower, and she was a modern-day Rapunzel.

Lee had learned how to piece her together like a familiar puzzle. Lilly seemed to fall in love with herself watching these videos. It was not in a conceited manner. It was more like finding a treasured possession after being convinced it was thrown out years before. She was beautiful once, and just maybe, she could be beautiful again.

The second video of these new uploads was a more polished version of the Sarah McLachlan sketch to replace the original. This was followed by a sketch where Lilly hilariously narrated her thoughts out loud as she tried on different clothing/makeup combinations for a blind date, only to receive a cancellation notice after she found the right combination.

The next several videos uploaded featured both single-sketch and two-person sketches with Lee as her co-star. Lee was always there to play the reactionary character who dealt with the fun chaos brought on by Lilly's arsenal of characters. By the time they uploaded the tenth sketch, they took an inventory of how many people were following her on YouTube. It totaled four: Frank, Jackie, Lee, and Judy.

Lee decided to print fliers and posters promoting Lilly's channel and posted them around the Second City theatre. For better or worse, Lee was known there, and had the marketing influence to get viewed, no matter how lame his productions sometimes were. He knew how to make the silliest of premises sell as if they were *Gone with the Wind*. Within a week of his posting information at the Second City and reactivating a Facebook account he had sworn off the year before, the inventory count of subscribers for Lilly's channel had jumped to forty-five.

Lee knew the missing piece to make that number grow to its highest potential. The viewers who were now following her story needed to see her take the next step. He needed her to perform live.

By the time they had uploaded their thirteenth video, it was that time. Though Lilly had a love/hate relationship with the number thirteen, she did not want to wait any longer to cross her bridge. Would she cross it, or burn it forever? She was growing anxious to find out.

Lee had spent the final day before the live performance directing every breath Lilly took. From her bows to her tempo, to even her articulation of every word, everything needed to be perfect in Lee's eyes. The respect between them seemingly grew as a real performance approached. Their quick insults and sarcastic commentary were replaced with passive-aggressive compliments and genuine half-assed efforts to listen to one another.

Before Lee walked out her door for the night, Lilly asked, "Do you still think my characters die at my feet? Remember? You said that a month ago. What's the status of those patients, doc?"

With his hand turning the knob, he turned to her briefly and said, "Purgatory. But the bidding war between Heaven and Hell is getting good."

It was Lee's way of telling her that she was much better compared to where she was a month ago. However, all of that could be lost in a flash with a terrible performance. Lee had told Lilly once, "It only takes one eye roll to kill a clown."

When Lilly went to bed that night, she slept wearing her lucky red clown nose.

The Binoculars

On the night of the performance, Lilly threw up sixteen times. She optimistically looked at this as a good sign. She saw it as her spitting out all her angst before the performance. She smiled back at herself in the mirror as she tried to wipe away puke from her quivering jaw with a shaking hand. She tried to drink water. It came up the moment her guests rang the doorbell.

Lee greeted Frank, Jackie, Judy, and Beth loudly to distract them from Lilly puking in the bathroom. They could hear her, but they chose to play dumb, almost as a form of emotional support.

Lee knew how to play the perfect host. He served popcorn, pulled out everyone's seats, and even got things started with some casual warm-up jokes he had borrowed from his time at the Second City. After everyone was settled in, it was time for the moment Lee had been waiting for. The moment Lilly had been daydreaming about for so long.

Lee jumped behind the camera to make sure the camera angle captured her perfectly. He gave her a short introduction and played her normal walk-on music. As the opening chorus of "Tubthumping" concluded, the audience could see Lilly's shadow. Only her shadow. Then she slid her right foot out and forced her left foot forward. She gradually made her way a few feet closer to her own stage, looking like a human slinky, with worried eyes and a sad smile that would only belong at a funeral. She reached the stage. She stepped into her living room spotlight, which was blinding to her as the music faded to dead silence.

She stood frozen. Numb from the tips of her toes to her cheeks. Dead silence. She could hear the clown's last dying breath from Lee's metaphor. She was jealous of the dead clown. She wished she could trade places with him, and not exist in this torturous hell where she melted slowly under Lee's awkwardly placed spotlight. She slipped both her hands into her pockets. In one pocket, she clutched the rubber clown nose she had hidden for good luck.

She controlled her breathing and tried to speak her first word but felt too nauseated. The butterflies in her stomach were freezing to death as she could feel the cold water reversing the logic of gravity and working its way up to her throat.

She spoke as she felt a drip of her own sweat hit her hand from her chin, "Scene number one." The moment those words came out, she darted off the stage, into the hallway, and into the bathroom to deliver the loudest puke anyone there had ever heard in their life.

Lee and the small audience sat quietly, unsure of what to do. The silence was way too deafening for everyone to remain posed like sitting statues. Jackie moved ever so slightly to stand up as if she were going to check on Lilly, but Frank grabbed her arm and kept her down. Jackie looked at Frank in alarm, but immediately noticed his wink.

"Oh, I get it!" Frank began laughing out loud. The kind of laugh that elbowed everyone in the gut to be encouraging and laugh as well.

Everyone was laughing except for Beth, but when Lilly heard the laughter, her heart stopped feeling numb. She felt a beat. That was all she needed to stand up from the bathroom floor.

The guests went from laughter to chanting, "Lilly's show! Lilly's show! Lilly's show!" Beth again was the silent exception.

Lilly began to sweat a bit less, and her footing felt solid again underneath her wobbling legs. She could breathe. Her soul had a pulse. Her mind was young again. Her heart now carried her out to the light at the end of the hallway. It was not blinding this time. Instead, it was pulling her. Laughter made the dead clown resurrect.

Lilly hopped on the stage, and it all came back to her in the blink of an eye. She could not feel her body, or her deep breaths, or the sweat from the soles of her feet. That was what she was happy to have again. The numbness of the showtime adrenaline. She hadn't felt that in so many years. Just like that, she was back. She nodded at Lee and started over from the top.

Over the course of an hour, Lilly performed eight two-person sketches and two monologues. As the evening went on, the laughter was no longer just for show. It was all real. At one point, Jackie had tears in her eyes that could no longer be held back. Lilly could not tell if the tears were because the moment moved her, or because the jokes were written that well. Lee assumed it was the latter.

During Lilly's final bow, Lee made sure to zoom in on her face, thinking he could direct tears to gently fall down her cheeks. They did not. Had those potential teardrops been actors, Lee probably would have fired them on the spot.

The most important shot he could grab with his camera was the look on Lilly's face. A renewed look of confidence shone in her eyes. The butterflies had finally exited her stomach and gracefully flown away to play somewhere else in the universe.

At that moment, through the lens of the camera, it was as if Lee were looking at Lilly for the very first time. She looked different. She looked confident. It made her suddenly look flawlessly beautiful. He was turned on by her. It was the way she interacted with her guests after the bow. It was the way she owned the room. He never knew how sexy she could be until that night. Still, Lee would not even think about unlocking that part of his heart. That key had been buried in an unmarked grave a long time ago.

Frank and Jackie had each brought Lilly a rose. Judy had printed off a pretend playbill and framed it. They gave Lilly nothing but encouraging words with every thank you. She gave them nothing but her most honest humanity as her eyes finally began to tear. Lee managed to capture those nearly fallen tears, even though Lilly again never let them fall to her cheeks.

Beth was the cold air in the room that stood out. Not just after the performance, but during it. Beth never laughed. It distracted Lilly, but she was determined for it not to defeat her. She was able to remove Beth from her mind by imagining guiding her to the window like a host seating people at a restaurant. She imagined opening the window, like pulling out a seat, and helping her to exit out. From that moment, she did not see Beth at all for the rest of the performance.

Beth was the last to leave. She stayed around to flirt with Lee, during which Lilly pretended not to hear every ridiculous remark coming out of her mouth. At one point, Beth even dominated the group conversation by talking about a trip she had taken to Paris, once she noticed Lilly's Eiffel Tower painting off to the side. This night was supposed to be about Lilly, but Beth could not care less about that.

Lilly still could not get over the fact that she had let Beth into her apartment, but it was now time to say goodnight to one another. Lilly thanked her for coming. In return, she thought maybe Beth would have a kind word to say back. Even if it were fake, Lilly would take the courtesy. Beth helped herself to a few more dips of hummus before she handed off her two cents, which fell out of her mouth along with the cracker crumbs. "Not bad, Lilly. Keep practicing. You might get there someday."

Beth exited. Her words still present.

"Keep practicing? Did I look amateur?" she asked Lee with honest concern.

Lee shook his head, also helping himself to her hummus spread.

"I need words, not a slight shake of the head." Her concern remained.

He swallowed his chips and dusted off his hands. "You were fantastic up there. I don't think. I know. That's all that matters."

"Are you telling me that as a friend or as a director?"

"I'm telling you that as an asshole who hates to give compliments."

That was the answer she needed.

After everyone had left, Lee helped her clean up. He was very talkative about the show as they cleaned. He was full of compliments, both for himself and for her. The ones about her were the most beautiful music to her ears. After helping her clean up, Lee surprised Lilly by offering her a gift. She opened a box poorly wrapped up in the Chicago Sun Times newspaper.

Binoculars.

The music stopped.

"I know you like to sit by the window a lot. You can see the world better now. The zoom in quality is great." Lee could not tell if she liked his gift or not. "You like your binoculars?"

Lilly walked over to his camera, which was back on a tripod and recording, and turned it off. For his sake.

"Binoculars?" she asked him, confused whether this was a genuine gift or an idiotic ploy for the camera.

"You always talk about how you can hear the block parties down the street. Now you can see them."

"Binoculars?"

"You're welcome."

"I never said thank you for this."

"Well, it still feels good to give."

"It feels like shit to receive," Lilly said, tossing the binoculars back at him.

"What the hell is your problem now?"

Lilly was dumbfounded at how clueless he was as she continued with her grievance. "You know what a real gift would be? A framed picture of a pretend playbill from tonight. Or tickets to see a real show. Hell, I'm not a cliche girl who likes flowers, but damn it, even a cheap bouquet with an overlooked funeral sticker on it would have been more appreciated. You understand what I'm saying?"

"I knew I should have kept the receipt," Lee said to himself, not even listening to her suggestions.

"Actually, the best gift of all would have been a hug. I haven't had one since the one I got from Jackie five minutes ago. It was years before that."

Lee never knew what to do with their awkward silences. They always agitated him and made him feel defensive. Lilly waited for an apology. She never got it. Instead, what she got was a glare back at her.

"Everything I've done for you is a gift. My presence is a gift," Lee said.

"Are you fucking kidding me right now? You think your presence is a gift? Let me clarify our situation. I need you because I do not have a choice. And vice versa."

"Vice versa?"

Lilly continued, "Yes. You need me so your day doesn't feel wasted. Pointless. Mr. writer/director/cinematographer, who can't get a professional job, so he uses his equally pathetic neighbor to get some views on a YouTube channel. Congratu-fucking-lations if you think tonight's gonna get us ten more views! I'm still terrified of everything and everyone beyond my door! Not that you care! And what do I have to show for the emotional shitshow this whole month has been? A friend? A stranger who can spare me ten minutes without shoving a God damn camera in my face? No. A fuckin' pair of binoculars is all I'm worth."

"All you had to tell me was thanks, but no thanks," Lee said as he continued to sigh in heavy annoyance.

"I swear to God, if you sigh one more fucking time-"

Lee could not even let her finish the sentence. He had to pull his sword of words out. "I'm sorry, but I will sigh! Because I don't need this! You do! You know why? Because I can go outside! I'm not like you and thank fucking God for that! I don't spend hours drawing a picture of the sun while turning up the heat in my apartment. Every day I go out there and I drown in my own emotional shitshow, yes, but I jump in every day because I can! It's my choice! I could gladly be doing something else with my life, but I chose to stay here dealing with you and your fucked-up life!"

They were now face to face. Breathing in each other's breath. No fear.

Lilly blinked first, and said almost with delight, "I never realized it till just now. You're more alone than I am."

Lee looked down at floor, trying to resist the urge to grab her and scream vulgar obscenities in her ear. Instead, he simply lifted his head up with a nod and whispered back to her, "Remember this conversation when you're dying alone."

Lee grabbed his tripod and walked away. On his way out, he slammed the door so hard that it startled Lilly. Yet, despite her fists shaking in anger at her sides, she walked over to the door and collapsed in front of it. Pushing her forehead against the door, she couldn't help but miss him already. She began crying. She hated herself so much for doing so. In her anger, she slapped herself. Again. Harder.

On the other side of the door, Lee was standing in the hallway. His hand pulled back every time he went to put it on his doorknob. He turned around and stared at her door. Wondering if he had gone too far. Pushing himself not to care. Pushing himself to shut out the sound of her sobbing behind the door that was pulling him back. He convinced himself she deserved it. It was too easy for him.

Over on Lilly's side of the door, she now pressed the side of her face to the floor. She stared at his motionless shoes through the bottom crack. Maybe he was coming back. She stood up and wiped away what tears remained. She stood in a confident pose and waited for the door to open. She was ready to accept his apology. The next noise she heard was the opening and closing of his door instead. She again collapsed to the ground and began to cry. She again leaned her head against the door, and with her hands dripping down it like her tears, she whispered so pitifully, "Please. Come back."

* * *

One week had passed by. No attempts were made to speak to one another.

Lee was having coffee with Frank at his apartment. Typical Italian apartment from wall to wall. He had a picture of the Pope, next to a picture of the Blessed Mother, next to a picture of Sinatra. Below the three was a struggling thumbtack trying to hold up an overflowing stack of takeout menus. Below that, a heavily stained coffee pot with coffee from two days ago. Still being served "fresh."

"So, she didn't like the binoculars?" Frank asked with a subtle laugh. He already knew the answer.

"No, Frank, she was not fond of the thought. The logic of the gift made sense to me," Lee replied, with a subtle back-spit of his coffee into his mug. "This girl is a real pain in the ass."

Frank patted Lee on the knee, like a father talking to a son. "You're really in love with her, aren't you?"

"Do you listen when I talk?" Lee asked, as he was dumbfounded by his question.

"Sometimes, you're hard to follow. You can't stand her, but you spend all your free time trying to help her get back on her feet and out the door. You're either sweeter than we realize, or the most manipulative asshole on the block. Which is it?"

"It's a fair question but understand this could be something special for me. A documentary on an agoraphobic actress that makes her return to the stage. I'm sold on that premise."

"I am too, but you can't just take advantage of people for your own good, and then get upset when they struggle to be happy about it."

"I'm struggling to be happy every day. She doesn't own the copyrights to misery."

"Perhaps you're pushing her too hard?" Frank suggested.

"She knew what she was getting herself into when I proposed the idea. Yes, I'm helping myself, but that is ultimately helping her. That's how I see it. Because then she'll be back to performing at a theatre, or whatever else she considers living a normal life. I only care that she goes back to being out of the building. Then, and only then, will she leave me alone. When that happens, I can I finally write my novel in peace."

"What's it about?"

"I have no fucking clue," Lee said with honesty as he noticed Frank trying not to laugh. "But, maybe when it's ready to be published, instead of begging on my knees for someone to buy it, people will want to go read that book by that guy who made that film with that funny girl."

"But then you'll miss her. You miss her already. Why else would you be sitting here drinking this coffee and bitchin' to me about the girl who didn't appreciate your shitty gift?"

"Was it a shitty gift?" Lee asked, as if he were making a point.

Frank said nothing, but said much in doing so.

"It was a shitty gift," Lee finally admitted.

Frank again patted Lee on the knee. "Instead of talking, try listening. Seems like you've done enough talking and gift-giving for the time being."

Coffee With Cream

The next evening, Lilly heard a knock on her door. "Go away," she said, knowing who was behind it.

"I know you're upset, but just listen. Just listen, okay? You don't have to let me in. I just wanted—"As he began that sentence, he was surprised to see the door suddenly open for him to enter. He let himself in and continued. "As I was saying, I wanted to apologize for the other night when I, um, suggested that you would die alone."

"I'm not sure I want to accept your apology just yet. If I hold out, maybe I'll get a telescope." Her sarcasm was so perfectly delivered that Lee couldn't help but chuckle.

"I could bring you one. You can be like Jimmy Stewart in ... oh, what was that movie?"

"*Rear Window*," she replied.

"Right. You know the movies."

"Not all of them. Not yet."

She sat at her kitchen table staring back at him, implying she was done talking for now. The stage was all his. Perhaps it was his turn to sweat under the spotlight.

"I know I've alluded to this before, but when you first wanted to go outside with me, I felt that you were shooting for the stars, but got burned up on the way."

"It's not every day you get compared to the Challenger disaster. What

84

a great pick-me-up speech. You sure you don't need me to start writing for you?" she asked, humoring herself while also loosening him up for his next pitch to her.

Lee continued on, "You accomplished a big goal last week. Within one night, you transformed into a completely different human being. You stopped being your usual self, which is a good thing. You no longer looked like a pathetic, weak-willed child."

"I gotta tell ya, these compliments…you just know how to weaken a girl in the knees, don't ya?" She just loved to make fun of him and could not help it.

Lee didn't mind. He kept making mental notes to himself to write down her jokes at some point. She seemed to somewhat trust him again, and that was good enough for him to carry on, "I'm saying, I think it's okay to try again. This time, we'll make it an easier approach. We'll wait until it's late at night. Quieter. The first goal is to get through the front door. If you do not want to go farther, but you do get there, we'll call it a win. We'll stack up as many of those over time as we can. However, if you do want to go farther, then we get you to touch the light pole right outside. Next would be the curb across the street. I thought it would make for a great shot if we sat on the curb under that streetlight and we got to know you a little bit more." Lee sat closer to her and finished his pitch. "It's up to you how far you go. How far we go. Just take baby steps. Remember that Bill Murray movie where he had high anxiety going places, and the doctor played by Richard Dreyfuss kept telling him to take baby steps? What movie was that?"

"*Something About Bob*. I've watched it twice recently."

"Exactly. We need to get you a life," Lee said, playfully returning a shot at her.

"If I can make it that far, I might be able to go a little further. If that's the case, I know a place where we can have that conversation," she said with a reluctant thought. "Back when I was a lot better at leaving the apartment, there was this one place I always used to go to where I never felt overwhelmed. I was completely at peace there. I would enjoy my late-night cup of coffee, and then be on my way as if the world were not so bad after all. It is at the end of the block and around the corner. Have you ever heard of Vandenburgs?"

"I still haven't found time to wander around since I've moved in," Lee said. He decided to make his quick exit while he was still in her good graces. "I'll stop by in a few hours, and we can try it out. In fact, let's be optimists tonight. We're going to Vandenburgs."

Right before he shut the door she added, "Oh, I almost forgot. Wear black."

Later that night, Lee returned at nine sharp. When Lilly opened the door, she saw that Lee had his hands full. In one hand, he had his video camera. In the other hand, a delicious-looking blueberry pie.

"That's a nice-looking pie," she commented.

"It's a silly thing we used to do at Second City. If we have a shitty night, we can at least look forward to eating the pie. If we have a perfect night, you get to pie me in the face. I then have to stand outside your window and sing a song of your choice," Lee explained as he began recording.

"If that's the case, I will make it to Vandenburgs even if it kills me." She crossed her fingers and placed his pie on her nearby counter.

Lilly grabbed her jacket and closed her door behind her. Walking down the hallway to the stairs was easier than Lilly had expected. The practice had paid off. Her forward progress was halted once she reached Beth's door. Every time she went to take a step forward, she instead took a step back. Lee noticed her biting her lower lip in discomfort. As the discomfort grew, her legs felt weaker. She then squatted down and sank her head in between her knees. Her breaths were heavy.

Lee slowly squatted down beside her. He knew he could not offer her his hand. Instead, he offered his arm for her to grab. She did so. He pulled her up slowly.

They returned to her apartment.

"That was just a practice walk. Doesn't count. Pie in the face is still on the table," Lee said, stalling for a thought that would help her. One did finally come to mind. "Here's what we have to do. Number one rule of agoraphobia recovery, according to Google, is we need to make you confident in your safe zone and carry that confidence straight out the door. So, let us focus on that energy that made you fearless just the other day. Clear your head. Now, of all those movies you've had time to watch, pick out your favorite scene. Imagine it is a live performance of this movie, and you're an understudy. The main actress, who is a legend in her own right, can't make the show because..."

"She died in a volcano."

"I was going to say she was stuck in traffic, but your reality is much more to the point," Lee said, trying to get back to his thought. "Anyways, you have waited your whole life to do a scene like this in front of a live audience, and that audience is praying you're going to deliver. They are fidgeting in their seats, debating about leaving because you are not the legend they were promised. You walk out into the light, and you shock the shit out of all of them. Do that scene right now."

Lilly thought and thought until she decided on an answer. "Marissa Tomei. The courtroom scene in *My Cousin Vinny.*"

"Pretend I'm not even here," Lee instructed as he gestured for her to start.

Lilly seemed timid. She tried to bring herself to begin, but kept cutting herself off. She kept feeling the need to summarize a visual, and to explain her own interpretation of the character. After she cut herself off for the tenth time, Lee interjected.

"Instead of pretending I'm not even here. I'm not even here." Lee backed up, opened the door, and let himself out into the hallway.

Unbeknownst to Lilly at first, he left his camera on her kitchen counter.

He sat leaned up against her door and listened to the dead silence coming from the other side. Just as he was about to let himself back in, it happened. He could hear her at the top of her lungs acting out the full courtroom scene from *My Cousin Vinny*. He could feel the enjoyment coming from her voice. Inside this door was a soul kissing its own adrenaline. Her energy rose and rose until finally Lee heard the knob turn and the door swing open.

Lilly stood differently; she had that confident look in her eyes. It was the same one she had when she was performing in front of her guests. It was the look all actresses have when they nail one scene, and they are ready to carry the adrenaline into the next. She looked at Lee, nodded, tossed him his camera, and led the way.

When they reached Beth's door, she slowed down, but pushed through all the way to the stairs. She paused at the top and looked back at Lee with a smile. She had herself a plan. She began her descent to the bottom, quoting *My Cousin Vinny* the whole way down.

She now looked at the small space between her and the front door. Peaceful. She nodded at Lee and led the way. She proceeded cautiously, but only the forward progress mattered. Each couple of steps took a minute to complete, but she made it to the front door. A new door to lean her head on as her legs began to show a nervous shake.

She kept her focus outside a nearby window. She focused on the quiet street—empty sidewalks and parked cars—not even any foot traffic to worry about. She was able to control the fear and channel it toward the adrenaline.

"If you go, I go," Lee whispered behind her. He wanted to give her a gentle push, but didn't want to risk erasing the progress she had made.

She pulled out a pack of cigarettes from her jacket. She bit down on one and could almost feel the drag with the deep breath she took.

"Are those mine?" Lee asked.

"Not now," Lilly said, dismissing his comment. She then added, "On an unrelated note, if you're not ready to quit, I support your decision to wait."

Lilly pushed on the door and forced herself outside. She almost stumbled to the ground with her eyes closed tight. The fresh air almost knocked the wind out of her. With the tiniest peek through her eyelids, she saw the moon. It looked different. It looked much closer.

It was still a bit much. She curled up against the building as if a train were passing by. He noticed her legs shaking and her breathing getting heavier. Lee turned his camera off.

"What are you doing?" She had to ask, because he never turned his camera off. Even when he said he would.

He leaned on the building, facing her on her level. He spoke the first line of one of her favorite scenes they had written together. She followed his line with her own. Like a musician, she needed a comfortable and familiar tune to get her rhythm back. After they recited the whole scene together twice, she regained her footing and stood up straight. She nodded thanks to him as he turned his camera back on.

"You're about ten feet away from the light pole," he said, adjusting his camera lighting for night vision. He then voiced some encouragement, "Blueberry pie, Lilly. Blueberry pie."

Lilly moved slowly. Very slowly. She slid her feet forward as if she were on the thinnest of ice. At times, she closed her eyes to focus on the sound of a quiet night. The crickets never sounded so beautiful.

With her eyes closed, her hand made contact with the light pole. She looked like an exhausted mountain climber who had just reached the summit.

Again, Lee whispered to her, "Blueberry pie. Blueberry pie."

Lilly put one foot on the street, and ever so slowly the second foot. It felt like walking into the ocean with a blindfold. It was terrifying, but only for brief rushes at a time. No one behind her. No one in front. After five minutes of standing right off the curb, she pushed forward. Forward. Forward. Till finally she felt her foot hit the curb across the street. Lee right behind her.

Lilly rubbed the sweat on her face off with her sleeve. The cool fall breeze did nothing for her as she looked back at her apartment window, which now felt as distant as the clouds.

"Can we sit for a second?" asked Lilly, helping herself to the curb.

Lee joined her. "Last time you got this far, how long ago was it? Where were you going? What were you thinking?"

"Kitty corner from here there used to be a pharmacy. Five months ago, I tried to refill a prescription. I only made it as far as we are sitting. By the time I got here, I felt like I was intoxicated. Felt like I was climbing up the sidewalk. Before then, I can't honestly remember."

Lee tried to convey some sincerity, even though the camera would not catch him from behind the lens. "You're doing a great job. In fact, I will gladly give you a piggyback ride home after we get coffee if it helps."

"We've got to get a move on because they close soon. Also, when we get there, you must do me one favor. You have to say hello to someone when we arrive."

Lee was curious what she meant by that, but held back his questions as she rose to her feet and carried on.

Averaging a few feet per minute, they did manage to make it to the end of the block and around the corner to Vandenburg's. They had twenty minutes before they closed. As they stood outside the entrance, Lee glared at Lilly as she took the camera away from him to grab a shot of him looking at the sign.

"You failed to mention that Vandenburg's is a funeral home," Lee snipped at her.

"I didn't think that detail mattered," Lilly causally replied as she

90

continued to explain. "You love coffee. You love graveyard metaphors. I figured you would love this place. What are you worried about? Everyone in here is wearing black and looking miserable. You'll fit right in."

"You can't be serious. I'm not going in there," Lee said as he leaned up against the building.

Lilly now leaned against the building next to him. She gave him a smoke and continued her pitch, "I used to crash wakes all the time when I was kid. As I got older, I assumed the habit would break, but it never really did. What can I say? I love to people watch."

"You can't go to a fucking mall!?" Lee asked in the loudest whisper possible.

"The saltier you get, the funnier you become. I love it. Let that relax you. It relaxes me."

"Good for you. I'm still not going in," he responded.

Lilly thought for a moment and dug a little deeper. She hoped he would understand her rationale from a writer's perspective. "Sometimes we don't take life as seriously as we should. We're all guilty of assuming there's a tomorrow. You can take a lot for granted. People. Moments. You can't cheat time. Being here used to always remind me of that. That was when I did my best work. I think the both of us could use that reminder now." She watched him as he seemed to gravitate to her explanation. She playfully patted him on the back and said, "That half-assed grin is good enough for me! Let's go in!"

"No!"

"You have to!"

"Give me one legitimate reason why I have to do this for you!"

"Binoculars!"

"… God damn it." Lee knew he'd lost the argument and opened the door for her. Once they were inside, Lee paused and whispered to Lilly, "Didn't you say something about me having to say hello to someone?"

"Yes, but keep in mind I have never met him, but I know he died on Tuesday." Lilly pulled out the obituary page from her back pocket and said, "His name was Danny. He was seventy-four years old. He was a professional painter his whole life."

As they walked in farther, they passed a row of paintings done by Danny. Most of them were scenic paintings with the sun setting over a mountain. By the time they walked to the end of the line of paintings, it was time to go into the room where the viewing was. Only a handful of people remained.

Lilly leaned in and whispered to Lee, "Usually there's two wakes going on at once and it's easy to blend in, but there's only one tonight. With most of the guests gone, we need to make sure we agree on a story as to how we knew him."

"I really don't think I can do this," Lee said as his forehead began to sweat.

Lilly grabbed a nearby tissue and patted his sweat. She made sure he was looking her in the eye as she said, "You can do this. You know why? It's because you and I never say no. We're the fools that always say *Yes And*. That's what makes this the best reluctant friendship in the world." She tossed the tissue in the garbage and then smirked back at him, "And you're up."

He nodded and took a moment to think of a story for how they knew the deceased. He looked in a nearby mirror and said as he fixed his hair, "When they ask how we know the departed, we state our car broke down a while back, and he pulled over to help us. We got to know him really well in the brief time he was with us, and that's all it took to never forget him."

Lilly took a pause and nodded at Lee. "That's really good. Sorry if I look shocked."

"You should be. Put that bullshit face away." He said to her as she tried not to laugh at his snarky comeback.

They made their way into the viewing. Lee turned his camera off and hid it in his jacket. They made their way to the front and knelt before the coffin. Neither one was bothered by death lying beneath their breaths. They shared a moment of silence, and then made their way over to the widow.

Lee gave the sad stranger a hug and said in a soft, somber voice, "I met your husband once, a long time ago. He helped me when my car broke down. I remembered his name and recognized it in the paper. I didn't know him long, but long enough for me to know he was a unique soul. I had to be here, if nothing else, to tell you even strangers were lucky to have known him."

The widow smiled back kindly at his words. Lee had delivered that line with such believable sincerity. No follow-up was needed, but Lee continued, "I can only image the amazing things he is painting in heaven. Perhaps, right now as we speak, the lord is sitting for a portrait."

Lilly tried so hard to not laugh at that comment but snorted loud enough for all to hear.

The widow hugged Lee and whispered back, "Thank you."

Lilly, not sure how to follow that, simply nodded and added, "I never met him. I'm just here for the free coffee."

Lee's eyes nearly fell out of their sockets. He was breathless. How could she say that? Why would she say that? He turned to the widow, already feeling another terrified sweat breaking out on his forehead, and went to apologize. His words were cut off by sudden laughter. The widow found the humor refreshing and hugged Lilly, who was still chuckling from Lee's tacky dialogue. With her chin on the widow's shoulder, she winked at Lee to help him close his dropped jaw.

They then left the widow alone, made their way to the lounge, and grabbed what was left from the coffee machine. Lee grabbed a large napkin to help keep his propped-up camera out of view on the table.

It was peaceful and quiet enough for Lilly to sip her coffee, but she became timid as the long hand on the clock inched its way toward closing time. Lee hit record on his camera, which hidden underneath the large napkin, and proceeded with his interview with Lilly.

Lee first asked, "How did you know the widow would laugh at your joke?"

Lilly responded, "I know that look on her face. I could tell she had been waiting all day for someone to say something to her other than a condolence. Everyone brought sorrow and a card. No one thought to bring a sense of humor." Lilly sipped her coffee and giggled to herself, "I have to admit I'm jealous. I thought your line was much more hilarious that mine."

Lee agreed as he rolled his eyes at himself. Lee then asked, "Is the coffee as good as you remember?"

It was the worst coffee she had ever tasted. In trying to keep with the theme of humility, she responded kindly as she nodded with half a frown, "It's got character."

"It's bottom-of-the-pot coffee. It's closing time coffee," Lee said as he forced it down.

"There's poetry inside that kind of coffee. It's not too hot, but that's because you can't stay too long. It's not too tasty, but you never want to get too attached to something you can't take with you. On top of that, it's also bitter, which symbolizes having to say goodbye both to the life, and to the evening. Though we must part, a better cup still awaits tomorrow morning. Funeral coffee is underrated coffee." Lilly sipped her coffee, very satisfied with her metaphor.

Lee played along. "Anything poetic in these donuts?"

"No. They simply taste like shit." Lilly laughed as she tossed one in the garbage like she was shooting a basketball.

From the time Lilly had finished her apartment performance, till the moment she sipped her funeral home coffee, Lee continued to look

94

differently at her. There was something so admirable about someone facing their fears with humor - laughing while suppressing crippling uncertainty. He began to look beyond her poorly straightened hair and paid more attention to how she chewed on her lower lip when she got both nervous and excited. While coaching her characters, he would find himself stuck glancing at the slim curves of her body. Lee never thought he would think of Lilly as sexy, but he knew she could be. By no means was it in an obvious way. The essence of her beauty was like a puzzle that appeared clearly only in the fleeting moments when every piece was connected perfectly.

And those eyes. Vulnerable, yet desperately holding onto a naive confidence she worked so hard to obtain. It made her smile unforgettable.

Lilly looked around the room to make sure they were both alone. She then took a deep sigh and cleared her mind. "So, now that the camera is rolling, what questions did you want to ask me?"

Lee asked her a question he'd meant to ask her the first day they met. "So, take me back to the beginning. How it all fell apart. How did you go from performing on a stage in front of a live audience to being terrified to step outside your door?"

She gave the question serious thought and responded with another metaphor. "When you're a kid, school can sometimes be overwhelming. It's a like a job. You have deadlines, politics, and a whole lot of unnecessary anxiety in between. Then one day you wake up, and you have a 102 fever. Your mom calls you off school, and suddenly, you feel like the luckiest kid in the world. No school. No homework. No drama queens judging you as you pass them in the hall. It's just you, a blanket, a warm bowl of soup, and a wonderful void of time. It's the most peaceful, relaxing, safe feeling you'll ever feel. The world is allowed to forget about you."

"I used to get pea soup and ginger ale every hour on the hour," Lee recalled. "You're right, though. It is a very safe feeling when you are in your room, living under your blanket. That can't be the whole story though, right?"

Lilly finished her coffee and looked as if she were strategically playing her words like chess pieces. "I seem to have a fate that was custom-made for unique tragedies."

"How so?" Lee asked as if she were being dramatic.

She suddenly felt anxious. Her hands felt shaky. No nails to chew or pick on, she already tore them up on her way over. She thought back to her stage days. Whenever she had to deliver a long monologue, she always looked for something to keep her hands busy. She had drunk enough coffee, but decided another cup would fit well in this scene.

She stood up and took her time grabbing the nearby coffee pot. She then laid out her history as she prepared to refill her coffee. Slowly. "This story may seem hard to believe. I know I still don't believe it myself." She slowly tilted the pot and began to fill her cup. "When I was a kid, my mom killed herself and my dad by driving their car off a cliff. To tell you the truth, I got over that pretty quick." She paused to sip her coffee. It was too hot to sip, but she did not mind burning the tip of her lips. She felt she needed to pause to properly pace her miserable story. "My foster parents were wonderful people. However, that was not meant to last either. After high school, my foster mother died of breast cancer. My foster father died in Iraq."

"Wait. You're telling me that you lost two sets of parents? And this was by the age of..."

"Twenty-three."

"Holy shit..."

There was a silence interrupted only by the final drips from the coffee pot falling into her mug, which was already filled to the top. She continued as she added sugar, "I did have a therapist who did help me out a lot. He always lectured me about seeking out every challenge life gave me. He believed that our tomorrows are guided by the dreams of our souls."

"That's beautiful. Whatever happened to that guy?"

"He hung himself."

Lee's jaw slowly dropped. He had no idea what to say in response. He was simply in awe of her horrific story.

"You said something really true about life when we first met on the roof. Do you remember? You said no one is exempt." She still felt fidgety after adding her sugar and looked for something else to occupy her hands. She added cream and began to stir, even though she hated cream. "You're right. No one is exempt from the fact that on any given day there is so little that separates us from having the best day of our life and the last day of our life. On any given day, anything is possible. Some of us wake up to be millionaires. Some of us wake up wanting to put a gun to our head before we even know what's for breakfast. All it takes is God to blink, and that's it. That coin toss we wake up to every morning is something I find terrifyingly unfair."

"Yet, when I work with you, you seem like a glass is half full kind of person," Lee remarked.

"I know how to hide pain. An actor once taught me that there's three faces in theatre: the tragic, the comedic, and the one that hides them both."

Lee thought that was brilliant. Though still in a state of shock that her story was so tragic, he leaned in with a slight smirk and said, "Looking back, had I known this, I definitely would not have taken the reverse psychology approach with you on the roof."

She smiled back at him. What caught her off guard was how he smiled back at her. He was always one to look away when a smile was coming. This time his eyes never moved. They just gave hers a nod of their own.

He finally looked down and continued, "So, why did you stop

performing if it kept you going?"

She put her stirring spoon down. Both hands held the hot coffee mug tightly as she began what felt like a confession. She sipped her coffee with cream. Not bad. It eased her to continue on, "Life has certain voids that cannot be filled with patience, prayers, or any mental placebo one might have for grace. I was told good things take time, but I was not willing to wait." She took a quick sip of her hot coffee and clenched her lips as the burn traveled slowly down her throat. She took one more and continued, "When I was at my performing peak, I refused to go home alone. I wanted so badly to fall in love and be taken care of. And I let too many people get too close. But still, I kept my door open hoping the next one was the one." She added more cream to keep her hands busy. "If someone in the audience really laughed hard at my jokes, the truth is I fell in love with them harder than they fell for me. The more that happened, the more I became the person the cast would talk shit about when they went out for drinks after the show. It grew to a point where I couldn't focus at rehearsal. I could not remember my lines on stage. The only place I felt comfortable in this world was on stage, but when the audience began to look at me differently…when they knew all my secrets…" Lilly bit down on her lip hard to try and hold back tears. They couldn't help but slip down her cheek. She ignored them and continued on, "…when they knew what I looked like underneath my clothes…underneath my skin…the mask I hid behind was gone. When the audience couldn't bring themselves to look me in the eyes anymore …that's when I knew I had lost paradise."

Lee sat there stunned but feeling he could relate to the constant need to fill voids. Unsure of what to say next, he shifted in his seat. He tried to find any words that would do.

She continued on while he searched, "For someone like me, the world is simply a job I have no motivation to show up to. Yet, it's amazing how you can miss the friendships you never really had, even the fake ones where you knew everyone was pretending. More than anything, I just miss the stage. I miss that escape. But, I fucked up. That's my own fault." She paused and swirled her cup, looking at Lee. "I'm waiting for you to tell me I'm wrong. Which I wouldn't mind. You do have a way with words. You're the writer. It's your job to tell us tomorrow is going to be okay."

Lee placed his hand on her cup as he noticed her subtly begin to shake a bit and said, "I'm not going to tell you you're wrong. The world is terrifying. For all we know, this is Hell. But even Hell has its fair share of surprises. It also has its fair share of people up to their necks in it right beside you."

She could tell he was trying to sell his own thought in a smooth and deep tone. "Did you want me to flip the camera around? We'll take your bullshit response from the top?"

They both laughed. He shushed her when she laughed too loud, which only caused her to laugh louder. Shamelessly. He followed ever so slightly with his own laugh.

Once Lee regained a somewhat serious composure, he continued, "So, you turned every day of your life into a sick day."

"Yes," Lilly admitted unashamed. "I ask you though, and give this question some thought, was it wrong?"

Lee leaned into it, but deflected, "What do you think?"

"I asked you," Lilly said, hitting his fastball.

"I'm conflicted."

"Explain."

Without knowing it, Lee borrowed from Lilly's tactic of borrowing some cream to stir as he stalled for time. "We all deal with tragedy in our own ways, but you lost a lot of time. Years. You're going to look back on your deathbed and wish you had that time back."

"I needed to run away to survive. Peaceful sanity in a world that flips on itself every day with so much unpredictability was worth every minute if it kept me happy. It was my own little world, predictably boring, both pathetic and continuously odd, but God damn it, it was beautiful."

She anxiously waited to hear Lee's thoughts. He knew her better than anyone at this point. She found herself wanting his sympathy. His warmth. There was room for two underneath her childhood blanket.

Lee responded, "My instinct is to spit at that idea. I worked most of my adult life at a hectic restaurant where there is no room for crying or soft feelings. You take abuse from people, say thank you to the soulless, and hope they tip while they shit on your life. They don't. You carry on, believing God or Karma will leave the tip instead. They don't. You carry on. It's that simple. There's no time for hiding. You can hide once the grass grows above your coffin."

She shook her head with a grin, "You and the coffin and grave metaphors, it never ends."

"The meanings of life are sometimes stashed in metaphorical graves. Realizing that will turn anyone into a writer."

"I feel like you listened to a lot of Evanescence as a teenager," she said, and they both laughed at her follow-up thought. "But seriously, you wouldn't have done the same thing in my shoes?"

"In many ways we wear the same shoes. So, maybe. I'm only giving you shit because if the point of life is happiness at any cost, then you have me beat. By a lot. Slaughter rule in effect," Lee replied as he finished his coffee.

She saw through him just enough to ask, "So, if we wear the same shoes, then what's your void? I'm sorry, you probably wanted that in the form of a graveyard metaphor. What's the coffin you're still trying to bury?"

The look on his face shifted when she asked. He shook his head and said, "We're not interviewing me tonight."

Instead of backing off, she leaned in further. "Does it have anything to do with that pink photo album you swiped from me—"

He cut her off. "We're not interviewing me tonight." As he began to stir the cream in the coffee he had no intention to drink further, he moved on to his final question. "Not to switch topics too far off misery or graveyard metaphors, but if you don't work, how do you pay your rent? Utilities? Groceries? Toilet paper?"

"I don't wipe." When Lilly saw the look on Lee's face, she wished she were holding the camera. "Jesus, I'm kidding. The actual answer is my foster dad is a deceased veteran. His wife worked for the state and had a nice pension. They left all their benefits to their only child. I'm set for a while."

"But for how long? You probably don't know. You don't seem like the type to have budgeted—"

She cut him off with the answer, "Seven months and two weeks from now I will be broke and homeless." She saw that Lee wasn't sure how to respond, so she changed the subject by asking a fun question of her own. "I know we're not interviewing you tonight because you seem very attached to that large stick up your ass, but I do have a trick question for you."

Lee gestured her to go ahead as he pretended to sip his coffee.

"I always hear girls coming in and out of your place. Never the same voice. Always a different laugh. Which, to me, would lead me to believe either you're the smoothest Don Juan alive, or you're a bit of an addict. If the latter is true, and I think we both know it is, why haven't you tried to make a move on me? Is it because you respect me that much, or is it because you find me unattractive, and not worth the time? Or is it more of a don't shit where you eat type of thing? You've got twenty seconds. Keep in mind, there's no right answer."

He hesitated to answer. He knew any response could make her feel rejected in some way. The typist in his head handed him a good line, but just as he was about to say it, the widow walked into the kitchen.

She finished what was left in her flask, walked over, and put her arm around Lilly. She then looked over at Lee. "You have a beautiful wife. I hope you know that."

Sensing Lee didn't know what to say, Lilly stepped in perfectly. "He came out of the closet just now."

The widow and Lilly again shared a great laugh at the face Lee was making. Lilly stuck her tongue out at Lee.

When it came time to leave the funeral home, Lee and Lilly stayed in character as husband and wife. Even though it was all pretend, she loved feeling like she belonged with someone. She decided at that moment she wanted her hand to be held. The idea of having her hand held suddenly did not seem repulsive as it always had. Not if Lee was holding it.

As they prepared to leave, she grabbed his hand and placed hers in his. Although trying to pass as a married couple, they almost appeared more like a couple of nervous teenagers as they walked hand in hand out the door. The moment they exited, they looked at each other indecisively.

"I'll give you your hand back," Lee said, with an attempt at a playful tone.

"Keep it for a while." Lilly wasn't even pretending to not be flirting. The moment she saw Lee's uncertain smile begin to dip away, she jumped back in, "It'll help me get back home quicker. The quicker we get home—you get home—the quicker you can edit this footage."

Lee nodded in agreement and continued to hold her hand. Her thumb rubbed on top of his while they looked both ways before crossing. Had a car been approaching, Lee still would have walked right into it without noticing it. It was mentally exhausting for Lee to not act distracted with her thumb still rubbing the top of his hand.

Lilly felt her breath growing short. It was fear, but not the normal kind she was used to. This was different. It was the sweat being shared between their fingers. It was the warmth that came from her shadow sharing the sidewalk with someone else's under the corner streetlight she hadn't stood next to for the longest time. The last time someone held her hand, she had been a different person. It was a different life.

Lee dismissed emotions that may have warmed up to the feeling of her hand in his. He liked to write about romance, but the real-life paranoia of feeling trapped with someone always kept the emergency exits nearby. The more she rubbed his hand with her thumb, the more conflicted and agitated he felt.

There was a fleeting moment when his heart did try warming up. A feeling that maybe the current situation was not one worth stressing out about. When he looked up to glance at Lilly, his mind was glancing at a different girl. The last girl to hold his hand.

Now, he wanted to be left alone.

Lee finished his final shot of the night of her walking back into her apartment. She could not believe she had made it. She went to make herself a drink, but when she went to offer one to Lee, he already had one foot out the door.

"Hey, wait, where are you going?" she asked.

"It was a good night. We should get some rest," he said with his hand on the knob, already twisting it.

"Are you forgetting something, Lee? My blueberry pie reward. I even have a song picked out. 'I'm Just a Girl' by No Doubt." Lilly couldn't help laughing at the thought she couldn't wait to become a reality.

Lee's bitterness had taken over. He needed to drink it off. Alone. It was the only way to put the emotion of old bittersweet memories to sleep.

"I lied. I promise I'll make it up to you." Lee quickly let himself out and shut the door behind him.

Lilly stared at the door. She slowly brought herself to her knees, obsessed with wondering why he turned his back to her so quickly. Her heart grew heavy as she wished he would open the door and come back. Heavier and heavier. This was always her cue to cry. The tears never came. Sadly refreshing was this less pitiful version of depression. There was not sobbing this time, but it still hurt like hell. Her heart just had a breath of fresh air holding his hand, and just like that, it was shoved back into a dark attic, left to barely breathe as it resumed collecting dust.

In Lee's apartment, he stood at his kitchen counter with an empty beer and that closed pink photo album. The staring contest between him and the cover lingered, as his hands could not gather the strength to turn to the first page. His heart was just as shattered as Lilly's. No one would know or believe that, other than himself. That was how he preferred it. Only in his bitterness did he finally take the time to acknowledge what it must feel like to be her. He was pining over a memory, but her pain was in the present.

He could not open the photo album. He placed it back on the shelf. He grabbed his smokes and decided to go for a walk. When he exited his apartment, he could see Lilly's shadow on the other side of her door. He ignored it. He pushed himself past it as if he were walking through heavy rain.

Lee exited the apartment building. It was at the street corner where it hit him. He could not ignore how his own thumb rubbed against his palm as he pretended her hand was still there. He leaned against the streetlight, feeling as if he wanted to go back in time—to a time that was only an hour ago.

His cigarette was nearing its end. Something he could not see was pulling him back from walking away any further. He just wanted to stay where he was. He missed what he'd just had, and he could not even comprehend what exactly that was. He just knew for that fleeting moment when her hand was in his, before unfortunate memories came into play, he felt like a kid again.

Sneaking into the funeral home reminded him of being a teenager when he and his neighbor used to sneak out late at night to go hang out at the playground. They would stay out of sight by hiding in the enclosed slides. There they would share a beer and have deep discussions about life as they knew it up to that point. It was the adventures of the young and ridiculous that Lee missed so much. Tonight, he felt young and ridiculous. He had Lilly to thank for that.

Lee put out his cigarette and sprinted up the stairs for his camera and tripod.

Back at Lilly's apartment, her phone rang. She sprang up from the ground and cleared her throat as she saw his name on the caller ID.

"Hey. How does the footage look?" she said as she tried to sound casual.

"You didn't eat that pie yet, did you?" he asked.

"No. Why?"

A moment later, she opened her window to see Lee gesturing to her from the street that he was ready to catch the pie from her. She let it slip out of her fingers, hoping it would land safely in his arms. It splatted onto his chest.

Lilly laughed so hard the whole neighborhood probably heard it. Lee loved it. He smiled carelessly as he rubbed the blueberry pie all over himself like soap.

"Which song was it again?" he asked.

"'I'm Just a Girl—'"

"By No Doubt. That's right." Lee nodded.

He looked around and made sure that no one was watching. For now. He cleared his throat as he tried to remember how it started. He pulled out his phone.

"No! No music! It's got to be acapella!" she shouted down to him.

"I'm looking up the lyrics!" he shouted back.

"Oh! I assumed you had them memorized!"

"Why would you assume I have that song memorized?" Lee asked as he put the music on his phone on the lowest possible volume so that he could still hear it, but she couldn't.

Lee took one last drag of an already finished cigarette and began to sing as loud as he could. The most ridiculous thing Lee had ever done in his life was also the most thoughtful gesture Lilly had ever experienced. She knew he had a heart. She couldn't help but fall a little bit more in love with it.

With blueberry still dripping off his face, he bowed at the end of his rendition. He then caught a flower that was thrown at him.

"Why, thank you, Lilly." Lee bowed again.

"I didn't throw that," Lilly said, looking around.

It was Frank. He was returning from taking garbage out to the alley and caught the whole performance. He applauded, much to Lee's embarrassment.

Familiar Faces

The next afternoon, as Lee was leaving his apartment, Lilly's door opened the moment his closed.

"I want to make you dinner tonight." Lilly posed this idea, which was immediately met with uncomfortable silence. Lilly, who suspected that silence might be his response, had a justification ready in her back pocket. "We've reached 150 followers, with most comments being supportive and not dipshit-ish. That is worth my famous pepperoni meatloaf with rice. I'll have it ready for six-thirty." Lilly jumped back into her apartment and closed the door before Lee could respond.

Lee was not sure how he felt about dinner. On one hand, he did want to talk to her about her next step in performing, which was a live-stream performance from her living room with a larger live audience. On the other hand, dinner between two people meant conversation. Casual chit-chat. The exhaustion of pretending to care. Lee knew how to play the part of the director. The part of being a friend was a character he could never play comfortably. As Lee stood there, still debating on whether he wanted to accept the offer, her door swung open again.

"Oh, I wanted to ask, if you could eat dinner anywhere in the world, where would it be?" Lilly asked, sticking her head out the door as if there were a secret surprise behind her.

Being late for lunch with his former Second City teacher, he cut the conversation short with a sarcastic answer. "I would love to eat dinner with the penguins in Antarctica."

Lilly just slowly nodded at him. He noticed way too many wheels moving in her head. He thought he'd better not ask. He went down the stairs and out of sight.

Lilly, heart filled with giddy fun, clapped to herself in excitement for a surprise Lee would be sure never to forget.

While Lilly went to work, Lee met with his former teacher, Ms. Murphy, at a bar just outside of the Second City. Ms. Murphy was an off-the-boat Irish woman and was the type that was always close to her students. She went out and saw their shows, and always bought them a drink after. It was her duty and a labor of love.

When she walked into the bar to meet Lee, she was immediately greeted with a free round. She knew he was going to pitch a favor to her.

When Lee was a student, he always bugged her for advice. She welcomed it at first, then after a while, she felt like she should be charging him for reading so many of his drafts. She never did. She pitied the fact that he never had enough confidence to know when his work was great.

Lee's pitch was long and drawn out. By the time she finished her third drink, Lee had just finished his first.

"You want me to bring my entire class to Lilly's apartment for the live stream performance?" she asked.

Lee insisted, "I think this would be a great learning experience for them."

"How do you figure?"

"They can see a former student of yours apply what you taught him about writing, sketch structure, and the importance of teamwork. Also, they can see first-hand how to *Yes And* when someone you're directing decides to mix Adderall and Merlot."

Lee could tell she was hesitant about the idea. She ordered her fourth drink and asked, "Are you actually helping this girl?"

Lee felt the answer was obvious, and asked in return, "Have you seen any of the YouTube videos?"

"Yes. I notice you use all my graveyard metaphors in your everyday life. Glad to see the weird ways in which I rub off on people."

Lee raised his new beer to her and took a drink.

She repeated her question, "You didn't answer my question. Are you actually helping this girl?"

"I know what you're implying. You think this is all one giant scheme to stroke my ego and get myself noticed, but it's not. Don't do this for me. Do this for her."

"That's still the same as doing it for you."

Lee just sat there tapping his fingers on his drink. He was looking for something to say that would correct her, but he could not.

She wanted to teach him a lesson, not in comedy, but in life. She squirmed a bit in her seat, as serious lectures were not her thing. "In our Writing 3 class, when I got back from chemo and resumed teaching, everyone in our class had brought in a card or a get-well gift at some point. Even a student who wasn't even in my class had bought me a miniature Fighting Irish flag. Sure, it was small as shit, and wasn't big enough to hang anywhere, but that wasn't the point now, was it? You were the only one who didn't lift a finger. Normally, I couldn't care less about stuff like that, but with you it hurt. It hurt because I knew you didn't know better. I thought that was incredibly sad. I know you have it in you to not be a selfish man. I think one day you can get to where you need to go, but you have to stop walking so fucking slow."

There was a long pause, and she could tell Lee felt both defeated and embarrassed.

She made the moment better with her reluctant grin. "Let me know when the show starts, and I'll wrangle them in for ya."

Lee was relieved. He had just guaranteed Lilly a packed audience, and one that he knew would be very supportive. He did not know how to thank his teacher. He tried to think hard about it as she began to catch him up on what was new in her life for a change. As soon as that conversation began, it ended the moment Lee's eyes spotted the girl at the end of the bar. He dropped a twenty on the table, which was short if he planned on treating his teacher, and simply noted, "I hope you can forgive me, but I have to say hi to someone. I'm not sure how long I'll be."

"It's alright. You take your time, and not a worry in the world from ya." Ms. Murphy smiled warmly at Lee as he left the table. She then whispered under her breath, "It's like singing to a deaf man."

Lee made his way to the end of the bar. There sat a beautiful, well-established-looking woman with auburn hair. She was too good to be in a place like this, but didn't mind standing out. She stood out the most to Lee. That face. It had been a handful of years since he last shared a pillow with it

"Hello, Alyssa," he greeted her sheepishly.

Alyssa looked at Lee in unpleasant shock. She tried to hide it, but it was too late to hide anything. A party waiting to get seated stood around her, blocking her escape. She couldn't even pretend to be naive and look the other way. She was now stuck in a moment she had gone out of her way to avoid in previous years.

She swallowed a deep breath as she anxiously tapped her fingers on the bar. "Hi, Lee."

Alyssa's story could be seen on her face. The way her eyes glanced up and down at Lee, she judged every inch since she'd last seen him. He looked terrible compared to when they were last together. She took comfort in seeing that. Her fingers tapping like a piano player made even the other patrons take notice. The grin was what scared Lee more than anything. Her grin had always been a default facial gesture when faced with unpleasant surprises that made her truly unhappy.

"You look nice," Lee said as the bartender poured her a glass of her favorite wine. "My treat."

"I'm just waiting on a pick-up. You don't have to treat me to a glass. I probably won't finish it." Though she said this, half her glass was swallowed in her first sip.

"How have you been? You been okay?" Lee asked delicately as he began to feel the familiar feeling of eggshells at his feet.

The worst memory of her life was what he was referring to. She took another extra-long sip of the wine and swirled what was left in the glass. Her eyes again glanced up and down to reassure herself that she was doing better than him. Only then did she have the confidence to respond. "I've been doing really well. I'm moving to California in the fall. Not sure if you heard, but one of my screenplays sold—"

"I heard." Lee cut her short. Too quickly. Expressionless, until he delivered a fake grin of his own. "You always wanted to go. I'm glad you're finally making it out there."

Lee pulled out the empty stool next to her and ordered himself a glass of the same wine. The bartender poured his glass, and then filled hers back up to empty what little was left in the bottle.

"The pizza's probably ready." She tried to cut the bartender off.

He responded as he kept pouring, "We don't have our normal kitchen staff tonight. All deep dishes are coming out late."

Lee inquired, "So, who is the deep dish for? I know you don't eat deep dish."

"It's for my roommate's friend, who is visiting from Texas. I was in the area, so I said I would pick it up." Her tone seemed legitimate. Lee wasn't going to press her on the details.

She felt obligated to ask how he was in return. "How about yourself? You still writing? I know after that one play flopped, you said you thought about quitting."

"I never said that," Lee chuckled, knowing that he did. "But yeah, I'm actually filming a documentary." Lee finally perked up now that the conversation had shown attention to his work. "I'm writing and directing for this actress who has a disability. I'm trying to get her back on the stage. It's been a long time for her. Here is her site. You should check it out." He handed her a napkin with sloppy handwriting on it.

"What disability is she suffering from?" she asked.

"It's kind of a multiple-choice answer with the correct answer being all of the above." And just like that, Lee's thoughtful allure had vanished quicker than a magic trick. Alyssa knew that train was never late.

Before Lee could go into further detail, a server came around the corner and dropped off her pizza.

"I guess the new guys are cooking pretty well tonight." She took another quick sip of her wine and started her escape. "It was nice seeing you. Take care."

"You too," Lee said back as he tossed the napkin with his handwriting onto her pizza box. "Don't forget to check her out."

She gave him a pretend look of interest as she slipped the napkin in her back pocket. He watched her make her way to the door, and within one blink of an eye, she was gone.

Lee felt anxious. He had let her walk away more than once before, but something was different about this time. He had always wondered what the moment would be like when he saw her again. He was still jealous of her. Worse than that, he never stopped being in love with her. Even though that combination made him sick to his stomach, he could not have this moment end over an unfinished glass of wine and a smeared napkin.

Lee ran out of the restaurant and down to the end of the block where she was walking. He had forgotten how beautiful she looked in the moonlight. Every argument, grudge, and unkind memory died in that moment. Lee let it all blow away with the breeze that was making her hair waltz above her shoulders.

"Alyssa!" he called out as he caught up to her. There was a moment of silence, and a nervous look on her face. He ran so fast to her that for a few long seconds he forgot what it was that he wanted to ask her. Finally, he found the first letter and the words came staggering out. "Can you do me a favor?"

Her eyes looked directly at his as if to ask if he were serious. With their history, it went without saying that his favors were used up. "It depends."

Lee took a deep breath and spoke his truth. "I know you're not happy to see me. I know talking to each other is the last thing either of us was expecting tonight. The last time we spoke—" Lee stopped when he noticed her shaking her head. He did not want her to run away and not let him finish. He carried on, speaking softly, with every word as unarmed as it could be. "Not everyone has gone through what we went through. I'm not here to dwell on the past. Actually, that's a lie. I am dwelling. We never gave each other a final goodbye, and I think that made everything worse."

"You still think you deserved one?" she asked, without any effort to sugar coat the fact he didn't.

"No. I know closure might seem like a pointless request. It's like digging up a corpse out of the grave just to change their tie."

"Still with the graveyard metaphors?" she asked. She then thought for a moment and went with a metaphor that she knew would speak to him, "I would have said it's more like hearing the most beautiful song be sung by the birds on the morning of your execution. It's nice and all, but if only you got to take it with you."

"I don't know. I live in the city now with the brown line right outside my window. Birds singing in the morning is a distant memory now. But, that doesn't mean I forgot how beautiful they sounded. Doesn't

113

mean I would just walk on by. I'm no good at playing deaf to a beautiful chorus I've heard once or twice before."

For the first time in a long time, she found herself just a little bit jealous that his metaphors were now just as good as hers. He had grown. Not enough. But just enough for her to want to stay for a few more seconds.

Lee continued, "All I'm asking is for a cup of coffee with you. It's not for my sake." Lee had to backtrack when her eyes called him out. "It is for my sake. I just always wanted to say goodbye to you the right way."

"I think you just did," she said, not even looking up at him.

"I need this. Please. You'll only understand if we sit down and talk." Lee noticed her contemplating and jumped at it. "There's a twenty-four-hour cafe I usually write at. Nice booths. Quiet. Delicious coffee always served fresh. Perfect place for an evening you don't wish to have."

She smirked at his wording. The forgiveness in her eyes still made him weak in the knees. Those eyes. He used to write for hours looking into them. He missed their kind, patient expressions.

He made his final offer. "Tell you what, you don't have to say yes or no right this second because I know you have to drop off that pizza. The place I'm talking about is called The Sip. It is one block away. I'll be there for the next couple hours working on some stuff. If you don't show up...well, that won't happen, because you always do."

She tried to hide a smirk as she went on her way. With that, Lee texted Lilly that he was canceling their dinner plans.

If only Lee had known how hard that text had hit Lilly.

Lilly had moved her kitchen table onto the stage in her living room. On top of the table were papier-mâché penguins dressed as little servers. Icicle lights that had been shoved all the way in the back of her closet waiting for Christmas time now dangled around the table, giving it a nice glow. The walls around the living room were covered from top to bottom with a freshly painted canvas. It was the most beautiful vision of Antarctica. Lilly even changed the bulbs so that they projected a cool light blue. At the end of the stage was a fan that was blowing out cut-up snowflakes made from carefully shredded newspaper page parts where there was no black ink. It was a mesmerizing display to be appreciated only by a lonely girl sitting by herself. She had made some of the wintery displays long before, but that wasn't the point. It was meant for two.

Back at the cafe, Lee grabbed a quiet booth and waited for Alyssa to show up. At first, she was just a few minutes late. Then she was half an hour late. Then she was a full two hours. Lee had arrived at 7 p.m. and ordered his first cup of coffee. By 10:30 p.m., he had polished off his seventh glass of their coffee-flavored wine.

The waitress walked by and handed him a bill, which was her polite way of saying he had been served enough. Lee did not protest. He paid his check and left.

He wandered over to a tavern about a block away and opened a tab. An hour later, Beth walked in with her friends and recognized Lee. She joined him at the bar.

"Flying solo?" she said, helping herself to a seat next to him that she assumed was meant for no one.

Lee just shook his head and slid her a shot he forgot he ordered. She took it. She felt intrigued by his heartbreak. There was also something about her intrusiveness that he found welcoming. They found themselves in a drunken cocoon with one another, welcoming each other's presence more with every shot they began to lose count of. They both found each other attractive, but only in looks. Their connection was still dead on arrival, which was only more apparent as they didn't comprehend at all how much they only talked about themselves.

After the bar closed, they walked back to their building. There was fake laughter as they tripped over each other's stupid jokes that neither one got. As they approached their building, Beth glanced up and noticed Lilly looking out her window at them. Knowing she was watching, Beth put on a production. She laughed as loud as she could, and even jumped on Lee's back for a piggyback ride.

They entered their floor, with Beth making sure everyone heard them arrive. They both entered Beth's apartment. Lilly couldn't help herself. She tiptoed down the hallway to Beth's door to overhear the conversation in her living room.

"What's the deal with Lilly? Are you two a thing?" Beth asked.

"No. I'm just coaching her," Lee replied with a slight slur.

"She definitely has issues. I give you credit for donating your time to someone like that. They need emotional help. I've tried spending time with her before, but there's a wall she puts up around me and it's very hard to break through. I just try to kill her with kindness."

Lilly rolled her eyes and flicked off the door. Beth noticed what she assumed was Lilly's shadow under the door.

"You mind if I use your bathroom?" Lee asked.

"There's a dollar charge," Beth said with an over-the-top flirty laugh so that Lilly could hear it. "It's second door on the left."

Lee went into the bathroom. Beth tiptoed quickly over to her door. She swiftly, but quietly, opened the door. She took one step out into the hallway and glared at Lilly. The two of them faced each other, motionless. Dead silence. Beth purposely waited until Lilly opened her mouth to talk just so she could cut her off.

"What the fuck are you doing outside my door?" Beth asked.

Lilly stuttered as she tried to improv a line. "I was…just…trying to… I was going for a walk, but I forgot—"

Beth cut her off again. Her threatening tone was so painfully condescending as she replied, "Honey, you suck at bullshit. Since you can't seem to find the truth now, let me hand it to you." Beth closed her door so that Lee could not hear her. "You're going to quit being a creep and go back to your apartment. If you don't, I'll call the cops. And believe me, it doesn't matter how fucked up you are, I will make sure they remove you from the building. Do you understand?"

Lilly was at a loss for words. She never had the strength to stand up to bullies like Beth. All she wanted to do was hide.

Beth continued with a softer, more passive-aggressive tone, "Honey, just nod and walk away. I'm trying to be patient with you right now, but I don't need you pressing your ear to my door as I fuck your neighbor."

Again, there were no words from Lilly. Just an exhaustingly painful swallow.

"You can go home now." Beth continued to lean into Lilly as she opened the door to let herself back in.

"Where did you go?" Lee asked as he re-entered the living room.

"Someone was delivering food to the wrong apartment. They're gone now," she replied as she poured a glass of wine for each of them. "Here. I've been meaning to finish this bottle."

They both took long sips and encouraged a stronger buzz to kick in before the hookup they both knew was coming.

"Going back to what I was saying before, I saw Lilly the other day in the hallway. She was busy practicing her steps. I helped her get down the stairs, but she didn't want to go further cause her anxiety kicked in. I just held her hand and kept telling her everything was going to be okay. Bless her heart. It's a shame what a mental disorder does to people." Beth finished her wine on that note.

Lee knew she was lying. Lilly never let people hold her hand. There was only one exception. The warmth of that moment came back to Lee as he looked down at the wine he swirled in his glass. Any sort of drunken, intimate mood Beth was trying to create died for Lee with that lie. This too was a moment of realization for Lee. Hearing Beth talk about Lilly made Lee realize how terrible he sounded when he described Lilly to Alyssa earlier.

Beth put her wine glass down and sat next to Lee on the couch. She put her arms around his arm and looked deep into his eyes. "You have pretty eyes."

"You stole my line," Lee said, with it intended to be more sobering and friendly rather than flirty.

"Write me a new one," she replied, now nose to nose with him.

Lee tried to think of something clever to say, but had become so drunk he could barely keep his eyes open. Beth had already felt her head become just as heavy. Not wanting to waste any more time, she moved in and kissed him. Again. And again. He did not kiss her back at first, but then decided to do so. With him now kissing her, she quickly got on top of him and moved his hands onto her bare breast. Before Lee could even process her movements, she began grinding on him with her shirt off. Next, she began to kiss him up and down his neck while she worked on loosening his belt buckle. The more physical she got with him, the less engaged he was.

She looked at him staring off and asked, "Everything okay?"

All he could see was the image of Lilly's hand resting in his. He slowly looked up at her and shook his head, which now felt like a bowling ball. Earlier he wanted nothing more than to get laid. All he wanted now was to go to bed. His heart was somewhere else. His mind was asleep. His pride and joy as soft as cotton candy.

"It's not you," he said as he gently guided her off him.

"I've heard that cliché before," she tried to say politely as she looked for a more honest answer as to what was going on. Her breasts were still in front of his face. She was confident in her sex appeal, but her ego needed answers. She grew impatient as she watched Lee look everywhere else but at her. "How about a raincheck?"

"You stole my line again." Lee got up and let himself out.

As he walked down the hallway to his place, he leaned on the walls the whole time. Lilly could hear him dropping his keys repeatedly outside her door. She told herself repeatedly not to go out there, but she couldn't resist. She opened her door and grabbed his keys for him.

He smiled at her, already half asleep. "Well, if it isn't that girl from that movie."

Lilly quickly found his key and opened the door. He was seconds away from passing out, but she managed to guide him to the couch before he did. She gave him a cover, put a bucket next to the couch, and made her way to the door.

With his last coherent breath, he blurted out to Lilly, "I didn't fuck Beth…I don't fuck liars."

"I believe the first part," she said back to him, but he was already passed out.

She opened the door but hesitated to let herself out. She turned around and looked back toward his bookshelf where the pink photo album was. It felt as if it were seductively pointing at her to come over.

She knew she was forbidden to look inside it. She wanted so badly to sneak over there and look inside, knowing that he would never know she had done so. Lilly knew what lay inside this photo album would reveal why he was so distant and cold.

She took three steps toward the shelf and paused. There was a moment where she felt she did not have to live up to Lee's trust in her, but she decided she would anyway. She took those three steps back, turned off the light, and left his apartment.

* * *

The next morning, Lee woke up late and more hungover than he had been in a long time. He could barely breathe without puking. He opened his medicine cabinet looking for any pill he could take for the headache, but it was empty. The fridge was empty too, along with his pack of cigarettes on the coffee table. He knew he had to somehow drag himself to the pharmacy.

As he made his way down the block that he could not remember walking down the night before, the birds began to sing. It was the familiar chorus he lectured Alyssa about the night before. Except now, it was deafening to him. Their melody was the most imperfect soundtrack to his pounding migraine. While stopping at a crosswalk, Lee looked over to a bird singing to him on a nearby fence.

Lee leaned in close to the unflinching bird and whispered to it, "Shut. The fuck. Up."

City Lights

Two weeks had passed. The rehearsals and the video shoots were quieter than normal. No energy to argue, but barely enough to perform more than one take. Lilly was still hurting from being stood up. It would be one thing if it were some random girl, but for it to be Beth was just too much for Lilly to stomach. She wanted to show Lee the dinner she had prepared, and the Antarctic skyline she had painted, but what was the point? To show him what he had missed? To show her own sweetness? Playing that card had always led to a losing hand.

Lee, on the other hand, never brought up that night. Apologizing might make him sound pathetic, and telling the truth might sound worse. In life, Lee felt he did not have any cards left to play. Yet, he always managed to find a way to lose without even playing.

Lilly's next big episode was scheduled for Black Friday. She was going to perform live in front of forty people in her living room, and it was to be streamed live as well. No outtakes allowed. It had to be perfect.

The Tuesday before Thanksgiving, Lee invited over a lighting and music DJ who had worked Lee's Second City shows in the past. He made her living room feel like a comedy nightclub.

During the rehearsal, every cue was perfect. Every line was delivered without hesitation or struggles with memorization. The two of them were perfectly in sync. The only thing that was lacking was pure joy in Lilly's energy. Lee thought she was too focused. Too tight. The best performances for Lee were those when an actress could make the audience laugh, but also show that she was enjoying the show just as much. Lee didn't see it. After the DJ packed up and left for the night, Lee sat Lilly down on the stage to talk.

She immediately felt agitated and asked him, "Why do you not look satisfied or happy with anything I've done tonight? You do realize I never once called for a line? I think that's pretty damn good."

"Yeah, it is pretty damn good, but I want it to be fucking great. You're somehow missing this," Lee said, tapping his heart. "Where did that go?"

"It's here. It's just exhausted," she said, easing her tone into a sad sigh.

Lee was growing annoyed with her sighs that had been present all afternoon. "What is this? Depression?"

"You're the only friend I have, Lee. If I were depressed, I would have killed myself the moment that set in."

Lee knew that was a great insult and honored it with a silent nod. He did secretly enjoy when she came back with great lines. He also took advantage of them as a great segue way to leave her place. Before walking out her door, he paused and turned to her. "Beth isn't coming Friday. She has plans with her new boyfriend."

"Why are you telling me this?" Lilly asked, pretending it didn't matter to her.

Lee did not say anything as he shrugged back at her. He closed the door. He knew how much she could not stand Beth. Perhaps, for all the hard work she had put in, she had earned a bit of good news. Lee and Beth were not a thing. It gave Lilly a new smile to hide away.

* * *

Wednesday night, Lee spent the whole afternoon hanging up flyers at the Second City that advertised Lilly's upcoming live-stream performance. As the evening approached, Lee left to meet Lilly at her apartment for the dress rehearsal.

There was a storm blowing through Chicago. The cold November rain was bitter and made commuting miserable. As Lee stood on the platform waiting for the brown line, he looked across the way at the other platform and shook his head at the funny timing of life. There was Alyssa.

Without hesitation, he raced down the stairs to cross the street, to pay for a useless ticket to board a platform for what could be an even more useless conversation than their last. He didn't care.

When he approached her, she could not have looked less thrilled. Had she been a depressed person, she might have jumped onto the tracks at that moment. He looked at her as she kept her eyes on the approaching train, the whole time pretending she did not see him.

He walked right up to her. "Pretending not to see me?"

"I see you," she said, without moving her head in his direction.

Her train approached, but he took one step closer between her and the train door. "Stay just a few minutes."

"I don't have time for anything you think we have time for," she said as she prepared herself to walk on.

"You're wearing yoga pants. You've got time." He paused a second to hear the laughter from the live studio audience in his head. "Another brown line arrives in four minutes. Please. I promise I'll never speak to you again in your life if you wait four minutes for the next one."

The train doors opened. She got on. Lee turned away and closed his eyes to shut out the door closing.

"Alright. Four minutes." She had gotten off at the last second.

Lee sat on a nearby bench on the platform that was barely protected from the rain by the heater above it. He gestured to her to join him.

She did.

He began, "You never showed up for coffee. I don't blame you."

He paused to let her get in a line. It seemed like the natural thing for him to do as a writer, but she was not interested in building a scene. She just wanted to get to the last page and exit.

He continued, "Had you showed up, all I was going to tell you was how proud I am of you. And also that I was sorry."

She nodded, but with annoyance. "I know all of this. It took me time, but this isn't news to me. Saying you're sorry now does not mean I'm obligated to forgive you and hand you a clean slate. I can't offer you any favors. Or friendships."

He nodded and accepted that. "I wouldn't take one. Pretending to be a friend is right up there with pretending you still love someone. And I know you tried to do both for me." He scooted closer to her and waited for eye contact before continuing. "I never meant what I said to you then. What happened was not your fault. It was mine." Lee looked closer into her eyes to reemphasize, "You did nothing wrong. Anyone would be lucky to have you. I just hope they treat you and admire you the way you always deserved." He paused for a moment. He did not want to forget to tell her why these better late than never words mattered to him. "We're writers. And life is a series of scenes. People move in and out. In and out. When people look back at us in life, we hope they remember us for our better scenes. I always knew that if life wrote a moment where I got to sit next to you one more time, I would at least tell you two things. One, I hope you have a great life. One that is filled with nothing but kindness, love, and more of these ridiculous-looking yoga pants."

She smirked at his comment and asked, "What was the second thing?"

Lee smiled at her and said, "I hate that you look unforgettable."

Alyssa smiled. It felt so different to hear this confession from a man who never admitted to being wrong. She nodded and tried to keep her stone face solid as she could.

"Is that it?" she said, as she looked into the distance to see if the train by chance was coming early.

"Nothing else. I'll leave you now." Lee got up and gave her a hug. "You take care of yourself."

Alyssa turned to walk away, but hesitated. She turned back to Lee and said, "You know why I didn't show up for coffee? I didn't feel the need. Not because I hate you. I don't, well, at least not as much as I used to. I looked you up on the channel you mentioned." After another quick glance behind her, she continued. No train. No rush. "The sketches were good. I laughed. You've really gotten sharp as a writer." She took a slight pause as she knew that was a gift-wrapped compliment. "I did always want you to find happiness. Just not with me. It did make me happy knowing there was someone else out there who looked at you the same way I once did."

"Who? Lilly?" Lee inquired, sounding oblivious to reality.

"She adores you, and you're such an idiot if you can't see that. Watch those scenes, the way she looks at you. That's not a character. That's her. She loves you."

"Trust me. She's not in love with me."

"I didn't say she was. I said she loves you. You don't have to be in love with someone to love them. Sometimes, you must begin by just understanding that. Where you go from there is up to you." She again peeked behind her at the next train, which was approaching fast. She handed him her last two cents. "Every decision you've made since I've met you has been for the benefit of yourself. It's always been about you. Do yourself a favor, and trust me on this one, don't make every God damn thing about you."

They both thought to themselves what last words were worth sharing as the squeaking wheels slowed the train to a halt. As the doors opened, she quickly pushed herself inside, feeling another goodbye hug would be too bittersweet.

"Good luck," she said as she nodded back at him. It was the simplest of gifts.

The doors closed before he could think of anything to say back to her. As quickly as the train had arrived, it took off again. Lee did not blink until the last train car had vanished around a building and was out of sight. With that, a part of his life was buried and gone forever. Though for him, it would always be a hollow grave. He sat back down on the bench. Still warm.

The rain had stopped. The crowd waiting for the train was gone. All was silent except for all the conversations of the past whispering in the wind. All their memories fading into a black night with no stars. Everything felt empty at that moment. Too quiet. If only she had not taken the rain with her.

* * *

Wednesday's dress rehearsal could not have been more perfect. The energy Lee had requested from Lilly had returned. They both felt as if they had caught lightning in a bottle, and both took turns taking swigs. Lee paid close attention to Lilly as they rehearsed. He did not see what Alyssa had mentioned. He could not find any love or lust in her eyes. He even kept count of her blinks when he held eye contact with her for longer than he usually did. No change.

Midnight arrived. After finishing the last sketch, Lee sat on the stage while Lilly swung from her trapeze. Neither could think of one thing to say to the other. After Lee let out a casual sigh, Lilly broke the silence.

"Awkward silence. We haven't had one of those in a while."

"Well, I remembered how much you said loved them," he said, still counting her blinks.

"The best one was when we first met on the roof," she recalled.

"Not an easy evening to forget."

"Sounds like you've tried. What would you have done if I had jumped?"

Lee had to think as if he were performing improv. He finally settled on a line. "I would think twice before ever giving honest feedback again."

They both laughed. She still was not used to seeing him give her an honest smile. As a growing amateur in the art of knowing everything about him, she knew he wanted to say more, but wasn't. She caught his lips moving slightly, as if he were rehearsing a sentence in his head. He did it more than once during the awkward silence that now followed his joke.

"It's the gift that keeps on giving," he said.

"No," she replied. "This isn't an awkward silence anymore. This is chosen."

"What do you mean?" he asked.

"I know that look. It's the same look an actor has when he's in the middle of a good scene that he's killing but forgets the next line. It's that kind of silence. The one where you want to talk, but you're so nervous that you fuck up some of the dialogue, and now you're trying to find the best replacement sentence that still conveys what bullshit you're trying to pull off."

Lee again could be seen moving his lips as he tried to think of a response. "I'm a writer. The quiet kind. If I don't have the right words, I can't show you dialogue."

Lilly now counted his blinks and replied, "I'm an actress. The kind that gets drunk on ambiguity. Bring any dialogue. I'll show you the right words."

Silence. Just one blink. Both at the same time.

Lilly then broke the ice for Lee. "This silence now is an awkward silence. You're very generous tonight," she chuckled. "See, you don't have to spend money on binoculars for me to be entertained. You just have to show up."

Lilly got off her trapeze, crashed onto her couch, and turned on her TV. After flipping through a few channels, she came across Charlie Chaplin's *City Lights*. Lee, who was headed for the door like always, stopped once he heard the music. It was one of Lee's favorite movies. Lee knew the work of genius this movie was and felt compelled to make sure Lilly stopped to watch it.

"Have you ever seen *City Lights*?" Lee asked, now fixated on the TV screen. "It's a beautiful story."

Lilly just shook her head. She didn't want to say much in return. When it came to Lee, she never got much in return. She did not want to do or say anything that would spoil the look on his face as he retreated from the door to watch Charlie Chaplin trot across the screen. She simply turned up the volume for Lee and grabbed him a half-empty bowl of popcorn from the day before.

Lee made himself comfortable on her couch. As they both watched in silence, a dialogue title came across the silent film. It read, "Tomorrow, the birds will sing."

Lee whispered to her as if they were in a crowded theatre, "That's one of my favorite lines. Ever." For the first time, he gave her a full, genuine smile.

"Why?" she asked with much curiosity.

"When I was a kid, there was a birds' nest in the tree right outside my window. They sang every morning. Loudly. Yet, I found their singing to be the most peaceful sound. To me, it felt like God was whistling a tune to help me start my day. Sometimes I would just lie in bed for an hour and listen. Listen. Listen. It felt okay to dream a little longer. Out here, I never hear birds singing anymore. Well, that's not true, one bird sang to me the other day, but I was hungover and yelled at it."

"You yelled at a bird?" Lilly laughed.

"I'm not proud," Lee joined her in laughter. "But hearing birds sing reminds me of being a kid. It always feels like it wasn't that long ago." Lee paused a moment to laugh at Charlie Chaplin.

"You really miss being a kid, don't you?"

Lee nodded. "But, that's quite alright. Tomorrow the birds will sing."

Lilly studied his face like she had never studied anyone before. This went beyond counting blinks. For her it was almost like a silent character study. She thought to herself about Lee over the course of the movie. She wanted to share her thoughts with him out loud, but instead kept her voice internalized...

I know you, and yet I feel like I'm seeing you for the first time. You're broken, but trying not to be. On some days, the efforts are more valiant than others. Some days, not so much. So, what broke you? Your secrets can hide only for so long behind the face you put on. You're like a clown stuck in the rain. Sad for so many reasons. For when a clown is in the rain, you wish to help, but first you find yourself watching the painted face on the clown melt away. The melt is fixating. You can't look away. Perhaps it is the clown's best day because now everyone can see who he really is underneath. I too could use a day in the rain. I guess we're not so different after all.

This film took him back to his earlier years as a writer. He was happy then. He was wiser. Kinder. The pride swallowed easier.

Lee looked at Lilly in a way he had never looked at her before. Humbly. He swallowed his pride. "Why do you like having me around?"

"I can take one good look at your life, and suddenly, I feel that much better about mine."

He nodded with a grin as she playfully chuckled and smacked his arm to encourage him to laugh with her. Both knew that was a great line. He then let down his guard for once and smiled at her. "I'm proud of you."

129

Lilly was frozen in shock at first, but she did smile back. It was time to bring the clown in from the rain. Lilly pulled a nearby blanket over herself and Lee. She laid her head on his shoulder. Slowly.

He was frozen in shock like someone had punched him from behind. At that moment, Lee wanted to leave, but it was as if his younger soul had taken over. In her window, he could see their image reflected. At that moment, he saw what Alyssa was talking about.

In the final scene of the film, Charlie Chaplin accepted a flower from a blind woman he fell in love with. She paused and looked deep into his eyes.

Charlie Chaplin smiled back at her as his dialogue title popped up. "You can see now?"

She nodded back at him. "Yes, I can see now."

The scene went black. The credits rolled.

Lee and Lilly's eyes slowly glanced toward each other. No blinks to count. Barely any oxygen to share between them. Silence. It was becoming too deafening for Lee.

It was the first time Lilly did not appreciate an awkward silence. She grabbed some nearby Oreo cookies for her and Lee to share. She proceeded to dip hers in a glass of wine.

Lee tilted his head in intrigue. "You dip your Oreos in Merlot?"

"Does this really surprise you?"

"Touché. I didn't take you for a dunker," he said as he grabbed one. "I usually twist the sides off, and go right for the good stuff in the middle."

"You do you, but I've got the Oreo dunk down to a science. First, you pick your beverage. Milk is fine, but kind of boring. Wine is sweet and delicious. Scotch and Oreos I only do on Election Day." She then filled her wine glass, grabbed an Oreo, and proceeded to give Lee a guided tour through her technique. "After examining the Oreo and confirming there are no weak spots or cracks, you submerge ¾ of

130

the cookie into the wine for about three to four Mississippi's. Five if you're in a gambling mood." She then raised the Oreo and took a bite, savoring the flavor. She gave an Oreo to Lee and guided him through his dunk. "It's all in how you hold the Oreo. I recommend pinching with pointer finger and thumb. Then, when ready, descend at an eighty-degree angle until you are in position for the counting of the Mississippi's. After years of doing it, I can feel when its ready. I no longer keep a spoon by my side in case the whole thing breaks and sinks."

Lee raised his Oreo like toast. "Cheers. Let's give it a try."

"Careful!" she cautioned him as he began to lower the Oreo. "Dunking is key. You must be quick, but not too quick. You also can't slowly lower the Oreo like you're Terminator lowering himself into the lava at the end of *T2*. Hashtag I know now why you cry."

Lee took a bite and chewed. The look of disgust on his face made Lilly laugh out loud. Her laughter was addicting. It caused him to laugh out loud as well. Whenever one would try to stop laughing, it would cause the other to laugh even harder.

When the laughter subsided, the silence between them resumed. This time felt different. It was less deafening. She was also sitting a lot closer than she had been before.

"What kind of silence is this?" he asked her.

"The terrifying kind," she whispered back.

Lee felt short of breath. Then breathless again. He looked around the room for any excuse to change the subject. He got off the couch and walked over to one of her painted walls. It was of a giant window with the lights of London right outside.

"I always wanted to paint like that," he said, not knowing where he would go with it.

Lilly walked over to him, feeling flattered despite the fact she knew she was letting her guard down. Her heart was foolishly wide open,

131

but she stopped caring about that the moment she left the couch. She grabbed a nearby paintbrush and placed it in his hand.

She walked away briefly to gather a few colors and dripped them onto a palette. He appeared content with taking her direction. During their heated rehearsals, Lilly had dreamed there would be a moment where he had to follow her direction. She took her time.

She then stood behind him and whispered in his ear to close his eyes. That alone was enough for Lee's blood to warm up a few degrees. He could feel her dipping the brush and guiding his hand across the canvas. He had no idea what master stroke of art was forming in front of him. It paled in comparison to the warm breeze rushing into his ear from her breath. Again, and again, that warm breeze blew in.

Was she doing it on purpose? He wanted to think so. In this moment, he was that hopeless romantic teenager again. A euphoria came over him that had fled his existence for so long. It made him high just to stand next to her.

"Open your eyes," Lilly instructed as she let go of his hand to soak the brush.

When Lee opened his eyes, he saw what he had painted. It was two birds sharing a broken branch that dipped into a river that reflected the clouds above. It was a peaceful sky with a sun over the horizon. Lee just stared deeply into the painting.

"You look like you're overthinking this picture. Of course, you would be," she noted.

"It just reminded me of this story I once heard in History 101. The Continental Congress had assembled for a convention to put together the Constitution. George Washington had this chair that he sat on that Benjamin Franklin was always fixated with."

"How are you getting that from this half-assed painting?" Lilly asked with a laugh.

Lee laughed as well but continued on, "When everything was said and done, and the constitution had been finalized, someone came up to Benjamin Franklin and asked him what he was fixated on. He said there was this sun that was carved onto the back of Washington's chair. He always wondered if it was a rising or setting sun. After he signed the constitution, he concluded it was a rising sun." Lee then gestured to the sun in his painting. "Is it a rising sun or a setting sun?"

"You tell me. You drew it," Lilly joked, loving Lee's hatred for ambiguity.

Lee stared at the painting for a long silent moment. He had to overthink it. It was his nature. Lilly didn't mind. He couldn't decide. She knew the answer the whole time.

"It's rising," she stated, like a teacher enlightening a student.

"How do you know?" he asked as he looked for clues.

She grabbed the paintbrush and added the final clue. Musical notes above the birds. "Because the birds are singing."

The world, as Lee had come to know it, stood still. When he heard his favorite film being quoted back to him, it was the same feeling as waking up from a coma. In Lee's case, it was like waking up in a coffin with the lid still open. His mind was clear. His heart was finally honest with him. She was no longer just some actress he was humoring. She was his friend. The most beautiful friend he had ever had. The most honest one as well.

Lee looked deep into Lilly's eyes. Still not ambitious enough to kiss her, he pulled her in for a hug. That hug made Lilly want to cry. She held onto him after he had relinquished his hug. Her eyes whispered words to his speechlessness that only he could interpret. She wanted to be kissed. His eyes slunk down as he watched his feet, deciding which direction to go. He couldn't ignore the breeze of her breath once again softly touching his cheeks as her fingers grasped onto the sides of his shirt. She wanted that kiss. She was not letting go.

"What kind of silence is this?" he asked.

133

"The kind that needs to stay." She closed her eyes and moved her lips closer to his to kiss him.

She kept her eyes open only for a second to notice his eyelids flickering as he looked in another direction. It was almost as if he had never been kissed. She questioned to herself why he would act so nervous. She quickly realized why as his exhale now flickered out as well. When he was talking down to her, he had no trouble looking her square in the eyes. When it came to falling in love with someone, it was a different story.

She wanted to continue moving in slowly for that kiss. Instead, she dragged her lips across to the center of his cheek and kissed him there ever so softly. As she did this, she curled her arms around him and embraced him as she again exhaled her warm breath across his ear. She then returned her lips to rest on the center on his cheek. She left them there to remind him how soft they were.

Lee's eyes could not sit still and his shaky hands followed suit. She gently took his hands and guided them to her cheeks. Their eyes locked. Silence. One waited for the other to blink. Silence. No blinks. Their eyes finally closed when he pulled her in and kissed her. His kiss was better than she had expected.

Both, with weakening knees, held each other tight for the sake of staying upright. Once they collapsed into each other, neither one could keep up. She continued to sigh in his ear, knowing how much she made him melt. He in turn picked her up and carried her to the bedroom.

She had not experienced intimacy like this in the longest time. He took his time with every inch of her. He loved that she smelled like candy. She loved how he would put his hand behind her head to guide her forehead to be up against his as both exhaled separately. Their two hearts played throughout the night like two kids breaking curfew on the playground. There was a feeling of trouble being right around the corner, but they both blindly trusted tomorrow to take care of itself.

Lee stayed the night, which was something he never did. In Lilly's bedroom, illuminated by her seven lava lamps, their naked bodies rested side by side. Their breathing in unison. Her long hair like a warm blanket as she rested her head above his heart, listening to it beat. They shared funny stories. They completed each other's thoughts. The tips of his fingers graced hers. Lee thought about the random one night stands he'd had. No memories worth keeping. No poetry between the sheets. With Lilly, it was all different. There was poetry everywhere in everything. The words did rhyme to the melody of her sigh still brushing along his ear and down his neck.

She felt so safe blanketed within his arms. He gave her everything she needed, physically and emotionally. She loved him. She wanted to tell him, but instead went with the safer choice of a silent embrace. The perfect kind of silence.

* * *

The next morning Lee left Chicago for the day to visit his cousins for Thanksgiving. He was usually the black sheep at the dinner table, the third wheel around everyone's happily ever after. This year, that didn't bother him. All he could think about was the big night ahead for his documentary, and his leading actress.

He thought about her the entire day. He tried to involve himself in his family's conversations but was too busy trying to remember the feel of the goosebumps on her skin, or taste of her sweat as he kissed her whole body. What really took him away from reality was reliving all her exhales, especially the one that followed after she held her breath during those moments of intense pleasure.

Many times throughout the day, he began a text, but deleted what he assumed were stupid words. He assumed anything he would say to her would complicate things too close to a big performance. His silence felt like the safest bet. The holiday away seemed a legit enough excuse to not have to speak to the elephant in the room.

She thought about him the entire day too. She sat on her stage alone on Thanksgiving, wondering if he would come back early, and if he would knock on her door before opening his. Even a simple text saying those words Lee assumed were stupid would have been very welcome. She sat there alone, beginning to feel more naked than she had been the night before.

The parade was on her television, but she wouldn't have been able to recall one float that was featured. She sat on the couch the whole time, reliving the night before. She could still feel his fingers between hers. She could still feel all of him, and reminiscing about the night before made her wet before she even began daydreaming. The daydreams would help pass the time, but not before long the night had returned, and twenty-four hours had officially passed. No phone call. No text. No knock.

She promised herself not to overthink it, but broke that promise by refusing to fall asleep. She stayed up expecting the knock that never came, as well as the text that never arrived.

She still believed that tomorrow the birds would sing.

You're free to disagree, of course, but I don't like this. I don't think Lee would launch into a preachy "life is a series of scenes" speech or say anything vague/impersonal at all to the woman whose life he almost ruined, during this moment I don't think he ever actually thought he would have. Maybe make it more concise, like, "I never know how to end a story. But if this is our last scene together, I want you to know how very wrong I was, and how much I still cherish all of the good scenes." That would also tie in better with the prior sentence.

Showtime

Lee did not return until Friday night, shortly before the show began. When he got to Lilly's apartment, the DJ let him in. Lee saw that Lilly was on the side of the stage finishing her makeup. Lee, still torn over all the emotions from the past two days, took advantage of the slight distance and kept it. Lilly noticed.

She kept one eye on him as he set up his camera, organized the seating for the guests, and helped the DJ with the lighting. Every time he walked near, her heart picked up its pace just like it had a few nights ago. It paused in confusion, forgetting to beat every time he kept on going right past her. Finally, he spoke to her.

"Want to run lines?" he asked sheepishly as he purposely took extra time to organize his scripts.

She wanted to play the staring game with him like she had the other night, but there was no eye contact to play with. Instead, she just gave her response. "Sure, I think that's a good—"

Before she could finish, he cut her off. "Take it from the top of first sketch."

They did run lines, but Lee never stopped to do it face to face with her. He just continued prepping her apartment and moving around as he shouted his lines with his back to her. The only time he came face to face with her was to explain his idea for a funny way to introduce her to the audience. He wanted to tell the audience that she had a unique warm-up routine to begin shows. At which point, she would come out and pour three shots for herself, with the third shot being accidently thrown at Lee's face during a sneeze. She would then optimistically smile at Lee glaring at her, glance at the audience laughing, and say back to Lee, "Alright! They're all warmed up!"

Lilly nodded, still trying to pull in a hint of how he was feeling from in between his lines. It was torturing her. She wanted so badly to know what was on his mind. Was it her? What did the other night mean to him? What did it mean for them? How pretty did he think she was when she took her clothes off the other night? How pretty did he think she was standing in front of him now? She didn't know. She tried her best to ignore the lack of chit chat and wrote it off as pre-show jitters. She assumed he would come around once the show was ready to start.

The guests arrived promptly and made themselves at home as Lilly was in her bathroom staring at herself in the mirror. She was trying to grasp how she had gotten to this point where love seemed to be possible, and the walls around her felt weak enough to finally push over. She had difficulty tallying the good parts versus the bad. Which side would tonight land on? It was only up to one individual, and it would all come down to this one moment. Tonight, Lilly had to be perfect. Just as important, she wanted to be beautiful.

Right before the show began, Lee walked into her bathroom and closed the door. Lilly's heart was racing again, and this time, she felt faint. She knew this would be the moment he would kiss her again. She hadn't been this close to him since the other night. Lee took a moment to look Lilly up and down. She was the most beautiful she had ever looked in her life. Her entire life.

They looked into each other's eyes, and both began to smile at the same time. Both lost count of the nervous blinks. Lilly held her breath as Lee stepped forward. Nose to nose.

"I'm so proud of you." She spoke first, assuming she was opening a

138

warm door for him to walk through.

He put his hands on her shoulders. Lilly quickly licked her lips and closed her eyes for his kiss.

"Good luck tonight," Lee said without any inflection as he kissed her on the forehead. "Lights up in two minutes," he added in his serious director's tone. He walked out and closed the door.

When Lilly opened her eyes, a tear fell out. She looked at herself in the mirror and stared hard into it. All she saw was a beautiful stupid girl. It was a long stare. She watched as two more tears rolled down past her cheeks to dangle on the edge of her chin. Teeth grinding. She hated how he waited till that moment to break her heart. Why now? Why could he not kiss her when she made herself look and feel this beautiful?

She took the deepest breath she could take, followed by another. She looked down. She kept her head down. She watched as the tear that dangled off her chin jumped off and landed into the sink. She watched as another fell right beside it. Once the tears connected, they slid into the drain and out of sight forever. She was determined to let that tear be her last.

After all, that beautiful stupid girl in the mirror was still her hero.

With her head still down, she took two slow deep breaths. She raised her head and looked back at herself in the mirror. This time, she looked different. The sadness was now taking a back seat. The adrenaline of owning the moment was present. Another deep breath was taken. One more taken after that. Her heart rate returned to its comfortable pace. The butterflies, the nervous chills, and the anxiety that had always torn her to pieces now lay on the floor next to the initial teardrop that missed the sink, and therefore missed its poetic exit. Her fear lay dead and buried underneath that. Nothing was going to hold her back tonight. Nothing. Nobody.

When Lee introduced her, she came right onto the stage. No fear.

No hesitation. The moment her shadow touched the lights, the love and support in her living room was overwhelming; the applause from Ms. Murphy's class was deafening.

Lee began his opening bit. "Ladies and gentlemen, welcome to Lilly's show. If you haven't guessed by now, this is Lilly."

Lilly gave him a look and whispered to the audience, "If you haven't guessed by now, he's never hosted a day in his life." The improvised line delivered a great laugh.

Lee continued, "Anyways, before we begin the show, we performers sometimes have very unique warm-up routines to loosen up. Sometimes we play games. Sometimes we sing songs."

"Lee usually jerks off in a closet while humming 'Here I Go Again.'" Again, Lilly's improvised delivery brought out a big laugh.

While Lilly soaked in the audience reaction, she caught the embarrassed glare from Lee. He only knew how to take a joke when it was one he wrote.

Lee continued, "Lilly, do you have a warm-up routine before a performance begins?"

"I like to take three shots," Lilly followed as she set up the three shots for herself.

She took shot one. Shot two. Shot three. Lee braced himself for the shot in the face gag, but it never came. Instead, Lilly grabbed Lee's face and kissed him on the lips. As soon as the long kiss was done, she slapped him across the face.

"I'm all warmed up for both our comic and tragic scenes." Lilly then pulled out her phone for a quick glance. "Oh, I just got your text that we cut the tragic scenes." The audience's laughter grew to a greater height and then into applause.

Lee was confused and aggravated, but quickly threw it all to the side. Lilly was live in front of an audience, in front of a live stream, and already owning the night. He was willing to pay the price, no matter

140

how hard the slap. Within a few minutes, he had already gotten over it.

From the first sketch to the last sketch, she stole every scene, and the audience was in the palm of her hand. She had no slip ups. No errors. No dropped lines. She did more improv within the sketches than she usually did, but every choice she made paid off. Every line she said elbowed every audience member, and everyone collectively saw her magic. Everyone in the audience took the link for the live stream, and shared it on their social media platforms. From the live stream poured in an endless bouquet of compliments and shares from across Chicago. She was trending.

This was better than the sex she had with Lee. It was pure love, and not the illusion of it, or the uncertainty of knowing it could be pulled from underneath her at any given second. This new kind of tear trying not to slip down her cheek was one of happiness; she knew her world could have collapsed at any given moment in this night, but instead she gave the best performance ever in her life. Her entire life. And she did it with ease.

The people cheering her as she took her final bow was the kiss on the lips she never got. The kiss on the forehead was bowing next to her.

When the applause died down, she walked around and took time to appreciate the company of every individual who came out. Lee introduced her to his former teacher, to whom Lilly immediately tried to replicate her accent.

As Lilly continued, Ms. Murphy leaned over and whispered to Lee, "Not bad."

"Not bad?" Lee said, surprised, and then stuck up for Lilly. "I thought she was damn near perfect."

"She was. I was referring to you." Ms. Murphy winked and began to make her way out.

"Oh, before you leave, I wanted to thank you again for helping us out tonight." Lee handed her a wrapped present. Lee could see she did not want to take away from Lilly's spotlight. "Open it when you get home."

After the long procession of compliments from people she had never met made its way out the door, it was finally just Lee and her alone in the apartment. There was a long stare between them. Those had become a tradition by this point.

Lee too was high off the adrenaline of a perfectly executed successful show. It made him oblivious to his own wrongdoings. He walked over to her with a flirtatious grin on his face. Maybe he was going to kiss her this time. Maybe he was going to hold her and say he was wrong for not falling in love with her sooner. She looked so beautiful, and he could still feel what it was like to have her that close. Lee, being the selfish fool that he was, stepped closer to her so he could kiss her.

She didn't even have to push him away or put her hand up. She just gave him a look that stopped him in his tracks. "Don't."

He looked away as he began to feel defensive. "I meant to say more earlier, but I did not want to jeopardize anything tonight. I did not want there to be distractions. If you judge me by the audience's response to your performance, I think it is pretty clear I made the right decision. For both of us."

"The least you can do is look me in the eye if you're going to be full of shit."

He looked her right in the eyes. His were unapologetic. Defensive. That hurt more than she had anticipated. "Never mind," she said as she looked away from him.

The silence between them at that moment was way too loud for either one. Both fidgeted in place. Relief came in the form of indistinguishable noise coming from outside. It sounded like singing.

Lee walked over to the window and looked below at a crowd of a hundred people gathering outside the apartment building. They carried signs that showed support for Lilly, and sang "Dear Prudence," using Lilly's name instead.

"What is that?" she asked, too nervous to come to the window.

Lee looked out the window for her. He turned to her to describe what he saw, but he could not get the words out. He shook his head in disbelief, and then walked away from the window so she could look while he grabbed his camera.

It was a sight that made her numb with shock. A large crowd had gathered outside, cheering for her to join them. She had never had more than two friends at any given time in life. Now, there were a hundred strangers auditioning for the job.

"What do I do?" she asked Lee.

"Go to them," he said, his eyes widening as he looked at his phone. "Your performance went viral. Most of these people heard about your story for the first time tonight. From what I am reading, it sounds like they're here to take you out for dinner. The Greek restaurant you like two blocks from here is staying open late just for you."

Lilly dropped to her knees and put her hand over her heart to calm it down. She was so overwhelmed and touched. Life never looked this lovely, and when it seemed to, it was always just a dream. She pinched herself just for reassurance. "This is really happening."

"You're welcome." He could not have said it in a more conceited tone.

She hated that remark. She felt like she was starting to hate him. Instead of turning around to begin an argument while he recorded her, she focused more on the fact that no fear had set in with the idea of joining the crowd to walk outside. With strangers she had never met. Since her visit to the funeral parlor, she had stepped foot outside twice briefly to try and walk around the block, but hurried back both times when an emergency vehicle drove by with sirens blaring.

"Alright, get yourself together, we got another scene to film," he ordered, much to her annoyance.

She grabbed her coat and walked out the door. She never looked back at Lee. She assumed he would close the door on his way out. Her pace increased as he followed her down the hallway. She didn't care if Lee kept up. She was over him. Over the videotaping. Over playing the part of the dumb actress that would fall in love with her director. That script needed a rewrite, and now the pen was in her hands.

She made her way down to the bottom of the steps. Of course, who just so happened to be at the bottom but Beth. Lilly did not have time to play games; she had the surprise party of a lifetime twenty feet ahead of her. Without saying a word, Lilly walked right past her.

"Honey, you might not want to go out there. It looks pretty crowded," Beth said from a few steps above Lilly, talking down to her in more ways than one.

Lilly turned around, joined Beth on the same step, and grinned back at her. "You can go home now." For once, Beth was the first to break eye contract and walk away.

Lilly made her way out the front doors to the cheers of a hundred people, along with a local news crew that saw the viral story and wanted to catch it as a feel-good segment. Lilly managed to never see the news crew, but they managed to see her at her best. Her strongest. The camera captured a soul that was easy to fall in love with. Frank and Jackie emerged from the crowd.

"That share button is pretty incredible, ain't it?" Frank said, putting his arms around Jackie.

Frank and Jackie locked arms with Lilly and helped her walk down the block to the Greek restaurant. The large group of people looked like a peaceful protest as they marched together down the street. Lilly could not believe how many times she had to stop to take a selfie with a stranger from the crowd.

Some of the strangers recognized Lee from Lilly's channel. They all seemed to give him the same time of day. It was a subtle nod. No selfie. No verbal acknowledgment. On a few occasions, Lee could overhear a whispered criticism of how he was an unfair asshole to her. The more selfies Lilly took, the more Lee would turn off his camera. Protecting an imaginary weak battery was the excuse he used.

When they finally walked into the restaurant, all the servers and cooks stopped to applaud Lilly. Her table was ready. Her server anxiously waited to take care of her as he pulled her chair out for her. Lee tried to seat himself, but Lilly's table filled up quickly. Lee decided it would be best if he sat one table over to grab a good wide shot of everything.

Lilly was like a spoiled child on her birthday. Endless drinks and ice cream were all treated to her by people she had never met. The love in the room was like that of a family on Thanksgiving.

While Lee captured it all from behind the camera, he waited for his own moment of spoils. A simple compliment for all the sketches he had written for her. The simple acknowledgement of the exhausting patience it took to direct her. To do rewrites for her. To keep her on her feet when she wanted to quit. To convince her that her laugh was precious, and that the dreams that went with it were always worth never giving up on. That last thought made him pause...

That was when he realized he should have kissed her.

A girl who sat nearby asked Lilly, "Where did all these great characters come from?"

Lilly, who was still feeling angry at Lee, knew he could hear her, and replied, "You would be surprised how much you discover through improvisation, which was what I was doing for most of what you saw. It especially helps when what you thought looked great on the page just isn't good enough."

Lee stopped recording. He stopped living too for a moment. Before the insult, Lee was ready to swallow his pride. Now, all he wanted to do was spit it on her plate of ice cream.

Someone else from a distant table followed up and asked, "So you

145

created all those characters yourself?"

Lilly grinned as she knew his ears were burning to hear the next words spoken, but no words were. She shrugged and nodded innocently.

Jackie raised her drink. "Cheers to a genius!"

One gentleman who sat next to Lee asked him, "What's the deal with you and Lilly? Are you two seeing each other?"

He knew he was close enough for Lilly to hear him as well. He replied, "Not at all. I'm the director. She's just my actress."

"You must be proud," the gentlemen replied.

Lee responded shamelessly, "She's a true inspiration to everyone else like her who has a serious mental disorder."

She knew she was meant to hear it. She didn't react. She couldn't. The pain of those words landed like a sharp cut to the skin. For the first split second, there was shock and no pain. Then came the pain.

Everyone in the restaurant gave her another round of applause. What Lee did not notice was the look on Lilly's face. Beneath the smile she put forth was a quivering chin that could not hide the fact that she was hurt. It was because she hated Lee. It was because she loved Lee too. It gave her pleasure to know that she cut him deep with every non-acknowledgment, and yet, her empathetic heart questioned whether she had gone too far to make a point. The words were already out of her mouth and his. It was too late to question themselves now.

As the night went on, no one from the crowd gave a nod to Lee's writing either. The more Lee thought about it, the more he knew some of that was his own fault, not because of his selfishness, but because of his editing decisions. The vast majority of the footage uploaded to Lilly's channel did not have Lee in it. He focused solely on her. Her good takes, her outtakes, her breakdowns, and everything else she wore on her sleeve were uploaded. Lee was saving the footage of himself for the full-length documentary. There were to be two main characters for the film: an eccentric actress suffering from agoraphobia, and a determined heroic writer who saves her like Rapunzel. But this was no longer a fairy tale. She was no longer a trapped princess.

After Lee felt satisfied with the footage, he left the restaurant before the bulk of the crowd did. No one noticed, not even Lilly. No one cared, not even Lilly.

Back at Lee's apartment, he was two whole bottles of wine in. He uploaded the evening's footage onto his computer and reviewed the part where she insulted him. It hurt even more the second time around. He poured the final drops of wine into his glass, and then he tried to make an NBA-style shot as he tossed the bottle towards the garbage. He missed and it shattered on the ground. He sat back in his chair and stared at the broken glass. Too lazy to clean it up. Too tired to find a broom. Too drunk to remember he even broke the bottle minutes later.

Lee sat in front of his computer in his living room and stared at it. He pretended he didn't know what he wanted to do next, but knew the whole time what he wanted to see. He opened a video file on his computer labeled, "Fun Outtake."

In this video, Lee and Lilly could be seen laughing in tears over a joke neither one of them could deliver with a straight face. The more they would try, the more they would improvise around the punchline, leading to hilariously awkward lines that elevated the scene higher than they thought possible. It was a beautiful moment to watch. At one point, Lee froze a frame, and there he again saw what Alyssa had seen. It was the way Lilly was looking at him in this one frozen moment in time. He had thought she looked beautiful before, but it was nothing compared to now. He was now more in love with her than ever, and also, had never been more jealous of her.

After Lee had stared at her smile for long enough, he got up from his seat and staggered across his living room to return to his kitchen. He stopped as he pricked his toe on a shard of broken glass. He jumped back in pain and hit his back against the nearby bookshelf. A few of the books fell to the ground.

After cleaning the blood off his toe, he proceeded to pick up the books and put them back on the shelf. The last to be picked up was the pink photo album.

Though he had held onto this album, it had not been opened in years. The moment he opened the first page, his eyes immediately wandered away, realizing he was not as strong as he had thought to look back at these memories.

By the fifth page, tears had escaped him. The unwanted nostalgia from these photos was strong enough to paralyze the mind. He pressed his forehead onto a photo and let his deep breaths exhale painfully. He then punched the ground. Again. Harder.

By the time he reached the end of the album, a baby's sock fell out. His kissed it gently. He then held it close to his heart and collapsed to the floor.

As sobbing was about to begin, there was a knock at the door. At first, he ignored it, but the knock persisted and would not go away.

He went to his door and opened it, expecting to see his favorite misery. He saw a different face. It was Jackie.

"You doing okay, Lee?" she asked.

Lee tried to look at her with a sober face, but his eyes were just too heavy. He opened his mouth, and there were six sentences he could respond with. Two of them were very cliché. He passed on them and filed them away in his head to be written for a different scene someday. The other sentences were too emotional, and not his style. By now, half a minute had passed as he stood in silence. His mouth moved but crumpled against words struggling to be spoken.

"How about a cup of coffee?" she suggested as she let herself in. She stopped at the edge of the kitchen when she noticed the broken glass.

Luckily for Lee, she knew where his broom was. She grabbed it and began to sweep up the glass. Never once did she acknowledge the mess. After she had swept it all up, she carried two warm cups of coffee over to the living room, where Lee was almost passed out on the couch.

Jackie sat down on the opposite couch. "Here. Take a few sips. Then, I want you to vent to me."

Lee sipped his coffee, and of course spilled some off the side of this mouth. He tried to rub it off with his shoulder as he said, "Why do you think I need to vent?"

"I saw the way you were looking at her tonight. Only love can produce a death stare like that."

Lee perked up a little bit, as he always did when the conversation was about him. Always the writer, he stared out into space as he tried to figure out where his words should begin. Once he figured out his opening line, he jumped in and began, "I'm growing tired of the games life plays on me. Every time I develop feelings for someone, it is either the wrong person, or the wrong time, or it's the right person, but God wasn't paying attention." Lee paused momentarily to take a large swig of coffee. He still needed all the help he could get to keep his eyes open. "For example, every time I've written lines for an actress, and shit, did I write for many, I always fell in love with them a little bit. Always felt sad when the shows were over. This show is just about over. This time it hurts in a much different way. And the irony is so fucking hilarious, I only wish I would have written it myself."

"Sometimes, irony is a gift."

"For an optimist? Yes. For a pessimist? Maybe. For me? It's just life's pointless fodder trying to open my eyes to something I've been asleep to my whole fucking life."

"That being…"

"…A way out of being me." Lee sipped his coffee and continued on, "I only wanted to help her because I wanted her to go away. I

149

figured helping her was the best way to push her out the door. I mean, I genuinely hated every second I was losing in life trying to get her to focus on one fucking line at a time. Yet, she finds a way to be incredible. I always said if she could just get addicted to Adderall, she would be the best actress in the city of Chicago. Instead, I'm stuck with a pain in the ass, borderline schizophrenic, agoraphobic actress who eats Oreos and drinks Merlot before every scene because it's her good luck formula. I fell in love with a fucking weirdo. The best kind too. Brilliant. Unforgettable. Unapologetically unique. You've seen it. The way she creates an entire world around her within a matter of minutes, and yet takes an hour to pick out a pair of shoes even though she's not even leaving to go anywhere. How can you not fall in love with that?"

"And this aggravates you to no end?" she asked, chuckling at the humor of it all.

"I don't think I belong with her. And yet, I know I do. And yet, I know I won't. It wouldn't be fair for her if I know I'll never settle down."

Jackie got up and sat next to Lee. She took her pause and prepared her story. She too had acted once. "I don't think you should be scared to fall in love with somebody, even if you only think it is just for a few moments." Perfectly placed, she took a dramatic beat. "Three years into my marriage, I had an affair. I always took the same train every day, and every day the most handsome man sat next to me. For almost a whole year, we never spoke a word to one another, but I loved the jokes he would tell the conductor. I loved his laugh. Every morning there was a leftover newspaper from the early commuters, and I used to always laugh at the comic strips." Jackie took a short break to grab the coffee pot and refill Lee's coffee. "One day I mentioned to this man how lucky I am that the commuter who sat here before me always left the newspaper behind so I could start my morning off with the comics. The man looked at me with this mesmerizing smile and told me that

150

every morning, he got up early to buy a newspaper to place it in my seat before I had arrived. When I asked him why he did that for me, he told me that seeing me laugh was the best part of his day. We both called off work the next day and made love until it was time to go home. Two weeks later, he died in a plane crash."

"I'm guessing you never told Frank," Lee presumed.

"I did. He told me he did the same thing right before I did." She took a moment to let that settle in and continued. "We fought. We cried. We both ran away, but we both came back."

"Why?"

"Because some things in life are bigger than your worst burdens."

Lee was uninspired and responded as such. "As a writer, I tend to live in between the lines. I can tell the difference between someone trying to share enlightenment, and someone trying to write off the shitty thing they did. I mean, really, what's the moral of the story here, Jackie?"

"Love is never ideal. Happiness is never perfect. Misery always has a seat at the table, but never forget that it's joy that built the house." Jackie kissed Lee on the forehead and made her way toward the door.

"You didn't even have a sip of your coffee," Lee said.

"It's for her." Jackie smiled at a sobering Lee. She added right before she left, "You too, Lee, are unique. Unapologetic. The good kind. Try not to take so much pride in your misery."

Lee sat on his couch for the next hour and waited for a knock that never came. When he did hear Lilly come home, he pressed his ear against his door and tried to determine if she was alone. She was.

He put his hand on the knob of his door, but didn't turn it. His stubborn curiosity wanted to see if she would knock on his door. He feared that opening his door would make him appear too vulnerable and pathetic. Still, there was just enough buzz left within his growing sobriety to encourage him to swing open the door.

He did.

Silence.

He stared at her.

She turned slowly to face him.

Both were unsure of whether to let go or hold on to the anger the day had brought. They both stared in a silence that seemed to go on forever. Neither wanted to speak first.

Finally, Lee opened his mouth to talk, but nothing came out. Every sentence he thought about starting involved too many words. Too many thoughts. How could he just cut to the chase?

He decided to say nothing. He turned around and closed his door.

Lilly whispered to herself, "Bastard stole my line."

Depression

The next day, Lee watched on the television as local news channels all replayed the moment she came out of her apartment. They described it as a viral Chicago moment. Lee was the unaccredited producer, writer, and director of said moment. Just like that, she had achieved a level of local fame that Lee had dreamed about for years. He took solace in the fact that if people loved her story that much, they would love the full documentary even more.

Over the course of six afternoon Bloody Mary's, Lee edited all the remaining footage. He found the perfect frame to end it with. It was a shot of Lilly walking into the restaurant to the applause of the staff. As the frame began to fade out, he dubbed her audio over it. It was a quote from Lilly that she had said earlier in the film. "That's the best way to start off a dream...Say *Yes And*...oh the places you'll go before you even think to wake up." If nothing else was to be shot, it seemed like a decent shot to fade out on.

Lee felt he had a goldmine put together, and there was a lot of emotion that came with it. He was taken back to when they first met, and when they had last spoken. A reluctant friendship had taken them beyond their wildest expectations. And then some.

Lee pulled out a cigarette and made his way up to the roof. The sun was setting. The breeze was welcomed on this unseasonably warm

November evening. Lee stood near the edge of the roof and visualized talking to Lilly for the first time. They had not spoken to each other in twenty-four hours, but it felt like a whole year.

He knew he was at fault, the first domino to fall in a succession of unnecessary tip-overs. Had he kissed her and told her he was in love with her, they would be sharing this particular sunset in her bedroom. Surrounded by those ridiculous lava lamps. He couldn't help but laugh at the thought. He tossed his finished cigarette down to the street below, and then turned around to notice she had been sitting in the corner of the roof this whole time.

Lee was startled at first, but then took a brave step forward with a freshly lit cigarette.

Lilly just stared at him. No response. Barely any enthusiasm in acknowledging his presence. Lee offered her a cigarette, which she took after staring at it for a moment as well. She lit it, took her drag slowly, and exhaled out even slower. She looked deeply into his eyes until he slowly mustered up the courage to look directly at hers. Finally, she put forth a question. "What broke you?"

Lee scratched his head, not knowing where to begin.

She continued on, "I need to know. The only way I feel I will ever respect you as a person at this point is to know why you stopped being the person I know you used to be. A person I know you still could be if you weren't so fucking stubborn."

"How would you know who I used to be?"

"We're sad clowns, Lee. I know—"

"You know nothing."

She tapped the ashes off her cigarette. Calmly. Again, she looked at him until he looked directly at her. Only then did she continue. "I can see it. It's in your eyes, but mainly it's whenever I make you laugh. You always try to hide your smile away. Right before you do, you let your guard down. Just for a moment. I'm tellin' ya, for that one moment, it's

154

the best part of my day. It's because you leave, and a sweet kid takes your place."

Lee exhaled his cigarette and debated where he wanted this conversation to go. He knew she was right, and perhaps he did owe her the truth. Perhaps it was the least he could do. He relented a bit and added, "You're right. We're both clowns. We're both broken people. I think a part of why I don't want to laugh at your jokes is because I hate that you're someone who always assumes my broken pieces aren't as shattered as yours."

Lee thought he was holding the high ground, but realized he was wrong. She would not waver her stare or walk away in disgust. She would stand firm until she knew the truth. She continued her motionless stare.

There was a long, dragging quiet moment between them. Lee was not trying to be stubborn; he just genuinely lacked experience in sharing. He had given many "opening up" speeches that meant nothing and were crafted to perfection to camouflage his lies. He did not want this moment to be a lie. Always the writer, his struggle was that he knew where his words would end, but not where the sentence should begin.

In that moment, he still wanted to call her out for not giving him the proper credit at the restaurant. Yet, he reminded himself that he was the catalyst in all of that. He knew his wounds were ultimately not from her, but self-inflicted. He understood, finally, that she had been in love with him for the longest time. She might not be anymore, and he had accepted that. However, he did not want to make the same mistake he made with Alyssa.

Should this be the last time they spoke to one another, he knew he needed to leave her with the right words. A clearer understanding as to what happened. Why he changed. Expositional dialogue followed by a poetic goodbye. It was what writers like him were good for. If nothing else...

He stared out to the sky and rolled his mind back to unpleasant yesterdays. When he was ready, he started his narration, "Fate is a word I think about a lot. Fate, by definition, is knowing that your life is beyond your control. It's the road you're thrust upon. It's the cards you're dealt."

"It's the metaphors you're forced to listen to." She made fun of him with a serious face. She grabbed his elbow and gently pulled him down to her level. "Don't talk to me as a writer. Talk to me as you. You don't have to sell pain here."

He sat down next to her and tried to figure out the best way to begin.

Lee took a moment of silent reflection. He looked down at the ground until he was ready to begin his story. He then looked up and began, "Seven years ago, I was serving at a restaurant. Servers were assigned tables based on rotation for whatever parties walk through the door. One night, as we're getting ready to close, in walks a happy couple, and then a depressed girl with a brace on her neck. My buddy got the happy couple. I got the brace. Feeling sorry, I sat down in the booth with her, took her order, and even flirted with her. She had just been in a car accident not too long ago, and there was a breakup, yadda yadda. After my shift was done, I did not feel like going home. So, I took her out for a drink. There was something off about her, but after a shitty dinner shift a drink is a drink, so whatever. After six shots of I don't even remember what it was, I went back to her place. I don't come home that night. In the weeks that followed, this girl calls and texts me nonstop. Turns out this girl is bipolar, and a junkie. Then I get the phone call telling me she's pregnant. Seems impossible." Lee paused only to exhale his smoke while grinding his teeth at the memory. He continued, "I finally own my shit, and I agree to take care of her and the baby. She tells me it's going to be a girl. I go out and buy her the softest teddy bear she can put her little arms around when she arrives. As scared as I am about the whole situation, I could not wait to meet

156

her. As for the mother, she wanted me to marry her..."

Lee's cigarette had run out. Lilly pulled the dead cigarette out of his fingers and replaced it with hers. "Still a few drags left."

Lee took a deep one and then wiped away the sweat moistening his forehead. He continued on, "I told her how I honestly felt. I was not going to marry her. She asked me for money. I asked her for a sonogram that had yet to be shown to me. It was at this point she confessed to me that she faked the pregnancy that whole time." Lee took another drag. He took his time as he exhaled and watched the smoke float away into the sky to join more pleasant conversations in the world. Now would come the hard part of the story, and he made sure to pull out his last two cigarettes at this point. He offered one to her.

Lilly handed it back. "Keep it."

Lee put one cigarette back in his pack and lit up the other one. He continued, "I wanted to kill her when she told me that. But as furious as I was, a selfish part of me felt relieved, like I was off the hook. And yet, there was this fucked up feeling of disappointment because I wasn't going to meet my daughter. I know this sounds strange, but whenever I imagined having a kid when I was younger, I always hoped it would be a girl. Whenever I saw my neighbor playing with her dad, he always looked like the happiest guy in the world, like he could not possibly love another human being more than her. I would look at him and think that's what I want to be when I grew up."

Lilly found herself in shock as she noticed Lee's chin begin to shake and tears fill up in his eyes, indicating this story was not nearly over. She put her hand on top of his and nodded at him to go on. Her eyes, which had been glaring at him since he walked onto the roof, had shifted in demeanor. They were kind. He could continue once he saw their empathy towards him.

"Three months later, I find out she lied about the lie. A premature girl was born. After struggling to stay alive, she finally stabilized and was brought home. They called her a miracle baby. Shortly after she was brought home, the mother fell back into her old habits. She overdosed. The baby...my daughter...starved to death. They found her in her crib with her arms around the teddy bear I had bought her."

As the first tear slid slowly down his cheek, the tickle of it set him off. He jumped up, grabbed a nearby empty beer bottle, and whipped it across the roof. He screamed in agony and collapsed to ground. He cried as hard as a broken man could. He sounded like he was going to suffocate under his tears, his fists clenching hard and his whole body shaking with an angry chill. Lilly had no idea what to do. She wanted to get closer to him, but was scared when she deduced from his look up at her that he wasn't done telling the story.

Lee exhaled another drag and continued, "I think about her every day. I dream about hearing her screams, and me not being there to hold her. Had I not been so easily manipulated, I could have shown my daughter a good side of the world. How I wish I could have held her and whispered to her that she'll never have to cry alone like that. Instead, I'm left wondering what it all would have been like...the hugs that we never got to give each other...the ice cream at the park that never melted on our hands...the fact that she probably spent her last moments reaching out for a hand to hold. I have no idea if there is a God, but I hope he was holding her when she closed her eyes." Lee tossed his cigarette to the ground and rubbed his foot over it again and again. "Her life was just a glimmer. She lived and died in absolute fear because her stupid father fucked the girl at table nine, when he could have had the couple at table twelve, the sweet people who tipped $100 even though their food was made wrong. They just had to hold the door open to let her in first. But ultimately, what can we say? It's fate. It's life. You get dealt cards. And if you're a God damn idiot, it becomes life and death."

"So that was Alyssa?" she asked him. "The guy you knew, who did lighting at my apartment, was telling me you never got over this girl named Alyssa."

He turned to her and showed her an expression she had not seen from him before. Shame. "Alyssa was the fiancée I didn't come home to that night."

Lilly was surprised at how disappointed she felt with Lee. Even though she knew about his addictions and had seen plenty of girls walk in and out of his apartment, it made her nauseous to think she was in love with someone who cheated on his wife to be. Yet still, he was not finished.

"We were fighting a lot at the time. It just so happened she found out about the other girl at the same time as finding out she was pregnant as well." Lee could not look Lilly in the eye as he concluded the story. "She, being the eternal forgiver, tried to keep everything together, but it was too much. She lost the baby. Doctor said it was from stress. I knew it was my fault. All of it. But I put it on her." He hung his head and sighed so heavily. "I can't believe the things I said to her. She has the same nightmares that I do."

With that, he collapsed back down to the ground and wept. Lilly sat next to him and guided his head to rest on her shoulder. Her soft fingers began to brush away the tears that fell down his face. She was a rock for him at that moment. She was tempted to cry with him but held back. Instead, she held herself together. She held him tighter while her heart shattered. His truth was so painful to her. She knew she would never be in love with him like she was before. She knew she would miss that.

"After Alyssa left, there was such an empty space in my life. I didn't want to fill it with random sex because that's what got me in trouble in the first place, but when you're addicted to fucking like it's heroin, the only thing you can do is get a vasectomy and keep the line moving.

My life did not need any more delusions of love, or me thinking I was decent enough to pull off a happily ever after with someone who'd waited their whole life for one. I'd much rather go home." Lee lowered his head from her shoulder to her lap, like an exhausted child. "I spent so much of my life dreaming of ever after. Only when I had it did I realize how much I did not want it. The dream was fun. Waking up from it not so much. When we were at the funeral home, you asked me about filling voids. Did that answer your question? I write. I drink. I fuck. If I'm not doing any of that, all I see is Alyssa's face the exact moment she stopped loving me. And vice versa. Or I'm just left thinking about my daughter, and this pink photo album I've held onto. It only has a handful of photos, the only ones that were ever taken of her. The rest of it is page after page of drawings I made of all the things we would do together. I started making them in the very beginning. Before all the lies. I thought it would be special to then recreate the drawings with her as she got older with real pictures. I would put them all in that photo album. The drawings and real pictures would all be side by side. I would then give it to her one day to serve as a reminder that the ever after you picture in life...always starts with a dream."

Lee laid flat on the ground. Exhausted. His mind just about paralyzed. He just looked up at the stars. Every few seconds a sniffle could be heard from him. He wanted his tears to be finished.

Lilly silently laid next to him. She was torn between so many emotions. Disappointed, yet sympathetic. Sympathetic, yet also disgusted. Disgusted, yet also filled with pity. Filled with pity, but most of all ... somehow ... some way ... very humored at the irony.

It seemed like yesterday they were both sharing the rooftop, neither one caring about the other. Much had changed. Maybe they would be in love again one night. Both knew it was not going to be tonight.

Lee stood up and breathed as if he had just run a race. He couldn't remember the last time he'd cried for more than a few seconds. With his back turned away from Lilly, he did not see her put the red rubber nose on her face. She quietly stood up and walked over to him. She leaned her forehead on his back and put her hands on his shoulders. He turned around, now noticing the rubber nose. It gave him a much-needed smile.

"I promise I won't scream," she said as he laughed. They then shared mutual silence, with their eyes appearing to almost nod at each other. They both knew it was okay to be close and not be in love in that moment. She then took the rubber nose off her nose and put it on his, just to make him smile a little wider than he already was. He couldn't help but fall in love with her all over again.

She pulled out her cellphone and quickly swiped her fingers across the screen a few times. A slow song with a beautiful soft trumpet came on as she placed her phone on the ledge nearby. It was Louie Armstrong's "La Vie en Rose." She grabbed his hands and guided them where she wanted them for a slow dance. He went to take the clown nose off.

She stopped him. "Keep it on."

Lee and Lilly swayed together on the rooftop as the notes played on. She tried not to laugh at the face she could not take seriously now. That in turn made him laugh at her. She then pulled him in close. Heart to heart. Cheek to cheek. Both processing each other's stories of wrong turns on broken roads.

The look on her face that he couldn't see was one of deep thought. Lee had a cautious face as well. As the melody continued, though, they stopped asking themselves questions inside their own heads. They just let the music do the talking while their hearts lay on the ledge. In the swaying of their bodies together, both had more they wanted to get off their chests, almost as if they wanted to shout from the rooftop how much they wanted to fall in love completely and unapologetically with each other, but both silently agreed to save it for another time.

161

When the song ended, he took the nose off his face and offered it back to her.

"I want you to always hold on to it," she said as she took a step back. "Because it's magic."

Both smiled at each other the same way. Both with the same conflict. They both loved the person standing in front of them.

She hugged him and held him tight. She then kissed him on the cheek and whispered, "Goodnight."

She turned around and began walking toward the door. Before leaving, she looked back at him with an optimistic expression and said, "Tomorrow the birds will sing."

He stood there and watched the door lean on the rock that kept it slightly open. He now knew how it felt to be looking at a closing door, hoping it would reopen. She did not come back. He put the rubber nose in his pocket.

He stayed outside for a while. The song they had danced to was still stuck in his head. He whistled it as he looked out at the city in the near distance.

For the first time in a long time, he looked at the world with much kinder eyes.

St. Patrick's Day

Three months passed by. Much had changed in the lives of Lee and Lilly, but little was said between the two. They passed by each other from time to time with pleasantries exchanged, but details of passing conversations were quickly forgotten.

Some nights they missed each other. On other nights, the thought of knocking on each other's doors felt burdensome. Mixed emotions always came into play. Good memories made them wish to open their doors and walk over to say hello. The bad memories kept their knocking hands at their sides. Then came the nights when one of them felt lonely, eager to speak to the other. Pride in not being the one who knocked first became the downfall on those evenings. On other evenings, it was because Lee or Lilly now always seemed to have company over when the other did not.

One night, as Lee was reviewing the finished product of their documentary, a piece of paper was slid underneath his door. It was a playbill. Lilly had auditioned for a romantic parody-themed sketch show at a nearby theater that would premiere on Valentine's Day. She wrote on the back of the playbill, "Do you have room for one more scene?"

* * *

163

She performed on a Friday night, and Lee sat in the back with his camera. He captured her first performance on a real stage in front of a live audience that was not seated inside her apartment. He could tell she was nervous at first, but she always knew how to find her footing in the spotlight. Lee couldn't believe how well she did, or how well-known and supported she was. There was no denying it. Everyone in this audience came to see her and fall in love with her. Lee captured them perfectly too in every frame. After she took her bow, he packed up his camera and made his way to the backstage area.

He wandered around a long hallway filled with many doors and open rooms. None of which had Lilly in them. With his camera bag strapped over his shoulder, he held a simple card in one hand and flowers in the other. He continued to wander around until finally he heard her voice inside one of the closed doors. He prepared himself to speak as he raised his hand to knock. He couldn't bring himself to do it. It was not pride this time. It was the sound of the actor inside the room with her. He could hear them kissing each other.

Lee had noticed their chemistry onstage during the show. He had tried to distract himself from it by adjusting his camera every time they shared a flirtatious glance at each other. He hated him without ever having met him. He hated that this stranger was probably the best thing for her. By now, she had made significant steps toward recovery. She was going out more and traveling further distances. It was only a matter of time until this happened.

Lee laid the flowers and the card on the floor by her door. He also pulled out a bottle of Merlot and pack of Oreos from his camera bag and placed it next to the flowers. He walked away and went home. When the door opened, the actor picked them up and handed them to Lilly.

She held in her hand Lee's card that read inside, "Bravo, kid. You've come a long way." Next to his written words was an illustration he drew of her with the red clown nose, screaming at him like she did way back when.

Later that night when she got home, she knocked on his door. There was no answer. She knocked again, hoping that maybe he was sleeping. Again, there was no answer. She stood there and wondered where he was at that hour. Little did she know he was in Beth's bed.

Lee lay there wide awake as Beth slept perfectly fine. He still relied on his old distractions. The feeling of meaningless intimacy was different now. It was painful. It was then in that moment, while he lay next to a pond of melted makeup and haystack of cheap hair extensions, he decided it was time for him to move out.

* * *

By the time a full month had gone by, Lee was packed up and ready to go. He timed it so that any heavy lifting took place while Lilly was at a rehearsal. It was easier that way.

The night before he was set to leave was St. Patrick's Day. He stayed in his apartment to gather the last of his things. In the morning, he would leave his key on the counter and be gone for good.

He had not told Lilly. He was waiting for the morning of. He was hoping he would have wise words for the occasion and needed all the time in the world to find them. He knew neither one would appreciate a long goodbye, but rather a nicely put bittersweet farewell till next time.

Lee finished the last beer in his fridge and sat in the middle of an empty living room. He reminisced briefly about the past six months, but tread lightly as to not drown in the deep end. What did not help matters was the knock at the door.

He knew it was Lilly. He just knew it. He chewed his lips, thinking of how to best say hello and goodbye at the same time. As the second knock came, he decided to just wing it.

"Hello, old friend," Lee said as he opened his door and smiled at her.

"Is it true?" she asked to get right to the point.

Lee nodded. "I would invite you inside, but I have nothing to sit on. Nothing to drink." After she revealed to him a six pack of beer and St. Patty's Day party hats she had been holding behind her back, he took a step back to let her in. "Aye."

They both sat in the middle of his empty living room. For a while, it was just long periods of silence featuring deep sips to polish off one bottle and move to the next. Never in fear of awkward conversations, Lilly broke the ice she wished she could have used for her room-temperature beer she'd forgotten to refrigerate.

"I'm thinking about getting married," she said.

Lee, not knowing how to respond, smirked and asked, "Destination wedding?"

"Fuck you," she laughed.

"I'm happy for you." He raised his drink to her before downing it.

She responded by finishing her drink as well. She then stood up and suggested, "Tequila?"

Lee grabbed his coat. "I thought you would never ask."

They walked down to the nearest liquor store together and brought back a bottle of Patron. They took shots and laughed about every shared memory they could think of. When the night got late, their goodbye to each other dragged out for a half hour.

Finally, Lee said goodbye and closed the door on her. Neither of them moved. Both noticed their shadows still present beyond the door. Lee walked to the door and wanted to open it, but instead leaned his forehead against it, with both his hands shoved back in his pockets. Lilly had done the same, except her hands were pressed up against the door and dragging slowly down in contemplation of what to do next.

Lee took a step back and rubbed his hands over his face in frustration over his indecision. He could not play games anymore. He swung the door open right as she was about to walk away. They locked eyes. It was time to mutually forfeit the games they had become professionals at. They threw their arms around each other and began to kiss.

At one point, Lee stopped kissing her and asked, "I thought you were thinking about getting married?"

"I was bluffing," she replied.

Lee responded by picking her up and carrying her into a bedroom that he forgot had no bed. Not that it mattered.

When all was said and done, they both lay naked with their arms wrapped around each other, wearing the heat off their bodies like a blanket. They both knew it would be best to just fall asleep, but instead dragged the night out, sharing a cigarette.

"What was your favorite sketch we ever did?" Lilly asked him.

He thought about a few of them and then told her, "I love the deleted scenes sketch where you and I kept acting out alternative takes of the same ending scene to a fake movie." He took the final drag from the cigarette she held and finished his thought. "That's what life is, though. Every moment is an alternate take to what your scene could have been. Should have been."

"How do you know which take is the right one?" she asked.

"I think, like any movie, you have to wait until the final credits roll. You look back at the story as a whole and pick it apart. Scene by scene, until your bag of popcorn is empty. If you would get right back in line to see the movie again, then I think the story is as good as it will ever be." He extinguished the cigarette and held her close.

She wanted to talk more, but could hear his breaths getting deeper and heavier. His eyes stayed closed longer, only to peek open by accident. She, however, could not sleep the entire night.

She wanted to be in love with him. Badly. When she pictured her future, she just couldn't visualize herself growing old with him. It was hard to explain, even to herself. It truly saddened her. The best way she could spell it out in her own head was that she knew there was a kind man lying next to her, but she did not want to spend the rest of her life searching for him. Justifying him. She wished they would have met as kids. As she saw it, they would have fallen in love with each other faster than the world could have kept up with. It would have been ever after. One that neither would have ran away from.

He felt the same way. He loved her, but it was time to go. That's why he left as soon as he woke up, as the sun was rising and Lilly had finally fallen asleep. It was closure until they would meet again.

Someday...

Someday

Over a year had passed. Lee's documentary, *Tragedy, Comedy, and Cigarettes,* had been selected for screening at a summer film festival in Arizona. The poster Lee had designed was clever. It had the theatrical faces of Tragedy and Comedy both smoking from a shared pack. The reviews from initial screenings were overwhelmingly positive.

Lee couldn't be happier to be attending. He had daydreamed about this day so often whenever Lilly would go off on some random dramatic rant during their days of filming. He would pretend to listen to her while imagining them both on a big screen to the sound of collective laughter and chewing popcorn.

When it came to his craft, the stars appeared to be lining up for Lee. Along with the premiere, he had finished the first draft of his novel. He was happy and at peace. He just wished he did not have to down so many painkillers to numb the discomfort he had been experiencing in his stomach the past few weeks. Just nerves due to the premiere, he assumed. He put on his best-looking face, and was curious if Lilly had done the same.

One hour before the premiere, he managed to find his way onto the roof of the theater, courtesy of a wrong turn and an unlocked door. The building was only five stories high, but the breeze at his back made it seem twice as tall. His eyes overlooked the entire town. He took the festival program that he had on him and folded it into an airplane. He watched it fly a surprisingly long distance until it glided out of sight.

"Let me guess. It had a weak thesis?" a voice asked back by the entrance to the roof. It was Lilly. More beautiful than ever. They mutually agreed, without saying a word, that it was good to see each other. They locked eyes. It was not a staring contest this time to see who would blink first, but rather it was as if they were reliving the night their eyes lay side by side.

"How long has it been?" she asked after finally blinking.

"Long enough," he said as he hugged her.

In a moment of unexpected silence, she resorted to making the same plane with her program. She sent her plane off. It did an upwards U-turn and crashed into the railing in front of them.

"Oh, the humanity," Lee chuckled as they watched it float slowly down to the ground. During the plane's long descent, he had a question he knew he wanted to ask the moment he would see her. He was hesitant to jump right into it, but as always, Lee hated awkward silences. Especially ones from long-awaited catch-up conversations. "I heard through the grapevine you're moving to London to teach improv."

"Looks like it. This guy opened up his own actors' studio and loved the idea of me being there to coach other performers. I guess he assumed my story would be a great marketing angle to get the studio attention. I don't mind. In fact, I love the idea of doing it. Classes don't begin until January, and performing in the land of Shakespeare has always been on my bucket list."

"You hate Shakespeare," he laughed.

"But, I love the land." Lilly joined in his laughter. She went to say more, but looked equally eager to keep it inside.

Lee knew what it was. "You're scared to get up there, aren't you?"

Lilly nodded. "I haven't flown on a plane in ten years. I wouldn't be flying out till January 1st, which means I have four months to get my

170

shit together. I feel like I'm looking for any excuse to back out, but I'm trying not to."

"It's not like you can take the bus, either," Lee said, trying to lighten her fear a bit. Seeing it did not do much, he just changed the subject. "I just finished the first draft of my novel."

"What's it about?" she asked.

Lee didn't respond. Whenever, he was about to, he kept cutting himself off. He had a story, but it was not ready to be told.

"Based off the stuttering going on in your head, I cannot wait to read this piece of shit." She laughed out loud and slapped his arm. She still loved to tease him. She then paused for a moment to shake her head at herself and change the subject. "I hope I don't look too insane in this film."

Lee put his arm around her and joked, "That makes two of us."

A few hours later, after cocktails and an intimate Q and A session with festival goers, the premiere of the documentary began. The lights dimmed. Lee and Lilly both glanced at each other with fingers crossed.

The audience loved the journey. They laughed with Lilly, both the agoraphobic actress on the screen, and the changed woman in the front row. They never laughed at her, just with. They cried whenever her soul fell to the ground, looking as if some of the enduring scars would never go away for her.

Lee felt so accomplished that the story he wanted to tell was now told. It was a tale of two friends. One was a struggling writer rediscovering his own brilliance. The other was a recovering actress rediscovering the stage and the world in front of it. Both reluctant to care about one another, but always finding a way to come through. This was the promised land they'd both dreamed of reaching. Flaws understood. Strengths perfected. Souls validated. Love … ambiguous.

During the documentary, Lee slid down into his seat and daydreamed of what he wished he could say to Lilly, if only he were the romantically transparent person he was as a kid. He visualized sitting in the same theater he was sitting in at that moment, only emptier, with only two seats in the place. One for him and one for her. He looked over at Lilly's face, fixated on the movie screen. He visualized himself standing up, walking around her, and saying every honest thought he could think of, with her never taking her eyes off the screen to look at him.

"Life is insane. I wanted my life to have nothing to do with yours. I meant it when I said I hated every time you made me laugh. And yet, I find it hilarious that now I would give anything for you not to get on that damn plane. I'd rather just lie next to you in the middle of nowhere. Between us, only the sweet sound of your stupid jokes. I'm going to love you forever. Just not in a traditional way with rings and promises, but rather through a bouquet of moments that will slowly fall to the wayside in time like decaying rose petals. I'm sorry, kid. That's just how I love. But that doesn't mean I don't love you. Only a fool wouldn't lose sleep missing you." Lee paused for a moment. He opened his mouth to say more, but decided to just stop and admire how happy Lilly looked. He then just sat back in his seat and slithered back to reality.

What Lee would never know was that while he was away in his dream telling Lilly all his confessions, she was in a dream of her own. In her daydream, they were in the middle of Paris. Right outside the Eiffel Tower. It was a rainy night, but they held each other underneath one umbrella. It wasn't big enough. Neither one cared.

She held him close as she listened to the soft raindrops hitting the umbrella above their heads and said to him, "I love you. Enough said. ...But you know me. I can't shut up even when I want to. Moments like this, I wouldn't have it any other way." She kissed him, and continued now whispering in his ear, "I really love you, Lee. I would have spent my whole life trying to figure out why and how, if only you had stood still. It would have been a good life. It still is. It's just the sunny days have more clouds in the sky than I would prefer, but God's flawed artwork is forgivable when there are nights like these."

After she said that last sentence, Lee tried hard not to laugh at the tackiness of it.

She caught him and playfully slapped him across the arm. "Fuck you. I was trying to be poetic."

"Please stop."

They both laughed. Even in a dream, she blushed.

"You're not a writer," Lee called out.

"It's my fantasy! I can be whatever the hell I want to be!"

Lee leaned in as if he were going to kiss her. Instead, he smiled and whispered, "Be you."

At that moment, an orchestra appeared behind them. All of them in tuxes. In the rain. Ready to play. She grabbed a glass of wine out of nowhere and saluted the conductor. After a long sip, she tossed the drink over her shoulder. On that cue, "La Vie en Rose" began to play just as it did once before. Only better. She then threw the umbrella to the side and forced Lee to dance in the rain with her. Of course, none of this was real, but it was the most fun she'd ever had.

When they were done dancing, Lee stood there looking at her, soaked, but feeling content because of what he wanted to tell her. Always the writer, his best smiles came when he found the right words, even if they were not his own. "Don't look so sad, like you're settling for an unsatisfied ending. The end is never the reward. It's the journey."

She grinned, now playfully calling him out, "I've heard that one before. Whose quote is that?"

Lee shrugged, "Some poet. Ralph Emerson, I believe. If I'm wrong, maybe it's Hemingway. Or Ghandi. It's definitely not Hitler."

"So, sometime between Jesus of Nazareth and Tom Petty, someone somewhere said it."

They both shared another laugh, which was followed by an awkward silence. It was the kind Lilly loved. She gazed at Lee through the rain and asked an honest question. "If we had the chance to do it all over again, would you do it differently?"

He took a step closer to her. He looked up and down her face and brushed his fingers down her cheek and across her shoulders. He then pulled her in and kissed her. When he was done, he kissed her again.

To Lilly, the kisses almost seemed to hurt. They felt like the kiss one would give when saying goodbye. Neither one had their eyes closed. She pressed her forehead against his.

He then gently let go of her and shook his head. Even in her fantasies, she could not force others to lie. She just stood there and cried as he grabbed the umbrella off the ground. He handed it back to her so that the rain would stop running down her face. "Even your tears are beautiful. Don't ever cry in the rain."

Lee then walked in the opposite direction and disappeared as the rain now poured down harder.

Both were awakened from their dreams by loud laughter coming from the audience. They were in love with the scene where Lee sang "I'm Just a Girl." At this moment, Lee felt his phone vibrate. He quietly made his way to the exit.

He went outside and found a nice, quiet bench to sit down and receive updated news from his doctor. The call was regarding his recent stomach pains. When the call was done, he turned his phone off and stared up at the clouds above him.

Lilly had walked out and followed him. She could see a look of dismay come over his face. She made her way over and sat next to him on the bench. They looked up at the same cloud.

"It's a poodle. A fluffy poodle. One that just jumped out of the bath and is trying to shake itself dry," she said.

"Funny. I could have sworn it was a hooker." He delivered his line well. Then there was silence. Lee finally went to speak, but Lilly cut him off.

"Everything okay?" she asked, gesturing to his phone.

"I've been having a lot of stomach pains lately. The doctors ran some tests." Lee wanted to continue, but just sighed a very deep breath.

Lilly stared down his silence. She tried to extract what it was leading to, but used her own fears to jump to the nearest conclusions. "Whatever it is, I don't want you to be afraid. If you're sick, I'll take care of you. I'll be right by your side. Like you were for me. London can wait." She grabbed his hand. "Lee, whatever it is, you won't have to go through it alone."

Lee still did not take his eyes off the cloud. He found peace as it moved away from the sun. The warmth of the light now covered his face. It was as if God had put a hand on his shoulder. He just blinked slowly and proceeded with his classic sigh. "I'm not dying. The doctor said everything is going to be fine. Just stress."

Lilly exhaled deeply, and then began to shake her head. "Well, that's a shame. I had a whole *Tuesdays with Morrie* sequel planned in my head. It would be called *Thursday Mornings with Lee.*"

"Just Thursday mornings?" Lee smirked.

"I got shit to do." Lilly delivered that line so perfectly that Don Rickles would have loved it.

They both laughed hard. They still fed off each other like it was yesterday.

After the laughter subsided, Lilly sat closer and placed her head on his shoulder, still with her hands holding his. She then pointed over to another cloud. "That's the hooker you've been looking for!"

"A little louder, Lilly," he said as they were both humored at Lilly's indiscretion. He then squeezed her hand a little tighter, wanting this quiet moment to last a little longer. "Everything about this day is beautiful. The only thing missing is those damn birds singing."

Lee and Lilly sat on the bench all afternoon. They leaned their heads on one another and played guessing games with clouds.

It was no rainy night in London, but it would do. I'm not sure what type of cancer you envisioned Lee having, but on the next page, you say it was stomach pains. It's probably good to keep it vague, but … I might leave chest pains out of it? Readers might think he got lung cancer from the cigarettes he and Lilly so often bonded over, and that makes the whole story a whole lot darker.

I think most likely colon cancer? That would explain stomach pain, and why he kind of appears to be wasting away. And colon cancer hits you silently and quickly. People will write it off as food allergies or something, and by the time they take it seriously, it's spread too far.

New Year's Day

After the movie premiere was over, they would not see each until the end of the year. They did send text messages here and there, but every get-together turned into a collection of rainchecks. For their own reasons, they preferred to keep their lives busy.

New Year's Eve, there was again a knock at Lee's door. This time, though, it was at his new apartment. When he saw that it was her, he knew just how to respond this time. He leaned against the door with his arms crossed and a jackass grin on his face. "Tell me a joke."

"Knock, knock," she replied.

"Who's there?"

"Honeybee."

"Honeybee who?"

"Honeybee a dear and open the damn door."

Both smiled warmly at one another as he opened the door. Every time they saw each other, not a minute had passed. They always looked better than they had the time before. Lee was an exception this time around. He appeared tired, run down, but still in good spirits.

"How did you find my place?" he asked. "Wait, let me guess..."

They both answered at the same time, "Frank."

"Figures. Are you leaving for London soon?" Lee asked.

"Tomorrow afternoon."

"Well..." Lee paused as he grabbed his coat. "Tequila?"

"Thought you would never ask." She remembered his line from last time.

He stepped aside and let her in for a moment. His place was much different than it had been before. It was peaceful and lighter in tone. There was no darkness to brood in. He had the curtains opened, as opposed to always having them closed at the last place. Where there had always been beer caps scattered across the table, there were now books on meditation. The pink photo album was nowhere to be found. He had moved on from memories he never got the chance to make.

The evening was young. They took a walk down to the corner liquor store and bought a bottle of Patron. When they came back to Lee's place, they made love three times before the bottle was ever opened. With a plane waiting for her the next day, they made sure to make it as passionate as possible. Both took their time with each other, and never even noticed that the year had changed.

When they finally got around to pouring each other a shot, Lee fell asleep. A deep sleep. When her usual nudging did not wake him up, she decided to take advantage of that.

She got up, put on one of his shirts, and drank her tequila in the kitchen. She found a piece of scrap paper and a pen. She wanted to write him a goodbye note before she skipped out for London. She had no idea when she would return. No idea when she would see him again. She had to take her time with the words she wasn't brave enough to say to his face.

She tried to push herself to wake him up. She just couldn't bring herself to do it. She could now perform in front of a hundred people, but still did not have the courage to tell one person how much she was going to miss him. She thought as a writer, he would appreciate a well-written goodbye note. This one with a clear thesis.

She wanted to write down every word that she had spoken to him in her daydreams. It broke her heart not to wake him and say everything to his eyes, but she was wise enough to know her goodbye would hurt worse if she did.

"What are you doing?" Lee's voice suddenly came from behind her.

Now was her chance to tell him everything. How much she loved him. She did not care that it was only from moment to moment. Imperfect. Stupid at times. To her, there was something beautiful about it being imperfect and stupid. Still, nothing came out of her lips. They were sealed. She just could not get the words out. Guilty of enjoying the awkward silence.

Lee knew what she was doing. A writer can recognize writer's block from anywhere. He gave her a wink and simply said, "Good luck." He turned around and returned to the bedroom. That was it.

She clicked the pen and began to write. She wrote for two hours before folding the note up. She walked back into his room, got dressed, and lay next to him for a few more minutes. When she managed to pull together the energy to leave, she rubbed her fingers through his hair one last time and kissed him on the cheek. She left.

She did everything she could to not look back. To not think twice. She squeezed the doorknob and swung it open and closed in a hurry. Gone. As far as she knew, it was forever this time. Fortunately, she had stopped believing in forever at a very young age.

* * *

When Lee woke up the next morning, he was hurt that he did not get to say goodbye to her, but then again, she was just returning the favor from the last time they spent the night together. He wanted to be upset with her, but knew why she did it. He also knew she was right.

Lee went to make himself a cup of coffee and saw her note sitting next to his coffee maker. He sat down and read it over. When he was done, he started over from the top and read it again. He read it repeatedly. Everything changed by the sixth time he read it through. He knew what he had to do. He had to go to her. Now.

Lee did not own a car, and if he did, he would not have enough confidence to drive into the O'Hare airport traffic. He made a call. Within a half hour, Frank and Jackie pulled up in their broken-down Chevrolet Silverado. Lee could have chosen an Uber but did not want to deal with the social anxiety of making conversation the entire way there. The familiarity of Frank and Jackie was good enough for Lee.

Lee jumped in the back seat with a pile of paper and a pen. He could talk if he wanted to; if not, he knew Frank and Jackie were fine keeping each other occupied. Sensing he knew what Lee's urgency was about, Frank stepped on the pedal as hard as he could.

"Jesus! Would you slow down!? You would think we just robbed a bank!" Jackie yelled as she added yet another unnecessary layer of makeup to her face.

Frank waved off his wife. "I'm trying to get him there quickly! I'm sure Lee would appreciate that, right Lee?"

"Yes, quickly, and alive on top of that would be greatly appreciated," Lee added.

Jackie couldn't mind her own business, watching Lee smile at what he was writing down. "Are you going to tell her you love her? Are you writing a poem? Is it a song? Are you going to sing to her? Frank and I can do harmony with you."

Frank added, "Is that what you're doing, Lee? We can record it. Maybe it'll go virus."

"Viral!" Jackie corrected him.

Lee just laughed and continued writing. His life made so much sense today. He had never written this quickly before. The words felt almost divine. Today would be his best work. He had to write the perfect ending to a story he had tripped face-first into.

180

Frank pulled up to the airport and wished Lee luck. Like a proud mother, Jackie gave Lee a good luck, lipstick-filled kiss on the cheek, which she then had to wipe off with her thumb. Once his face was clean, Lee took off inside the airport.

He bought a refundable ticket and made his way through security. The search began. To his surprise, what he assumed would be a nearly impossible task was so simple. He saw her right away. Whether she was standing at the edge of a rooftop, or in the middle of a crowded airport, he always seemed to gravitate to her.

She had not noticed him yet. She was too busy pacing in place, breathing heavily at the sight of the airplane pulling up right outside the terminal window. She began to feel like she was a child drowning at the deep end of the pool. No adults in sight. Absolute fear set in for her.

As they began roll call for seating, an unsettling feeling began escalating, one that she knew all too well. She felt a panic attack setting in. Her knees buckled. The most terrifying earthquake began, but only she could feel the world collapsing. She could not move forward. It was impossible. The only relief the moment could provide would be if she just turned away and ran with her head down. She viewed her failure as a noble effort meant for another day. Another year. Perhaps, another life.

She took one last look at the plane staring at her from outside. She turned away, only to be halted by the sight of Lee standing there. She knew, as well as he did from reading her note, that there was no way she was going to board that plane. He knew how to read in between her lines.

Suddenly, the earthquake died, and in its place was a feeling of utter safety. It was the feeling she had pursued all those years she hid from the world. She was once again a sick child underneath her favorite blanket. She took the first steps towards him, slowly, and he followed suit. They were face to face now. The airplane outside the window still stared at her, as if it were jealous of Lee.

She stared at him, almost to make sure he was real. She cleared her throat and smiled blissfully. "I'm ready to go home."

Lilly expected Lee to sweep her off her feet. She began to brainstorm how he could carry her away, while still dragging her luggage along. Maybe it would be best to just leave it all there and start over. She was ready to go home and be loved.

However, Lee just stood there. Expressionless, he just looked back at her without saying anything at first. For the first time ever, he enjoyed the awkward silence more than she did.

Lilly could not help but notice that she was not being swept off her feet. He didn't even throw his arms around her. He nodded with a very curious grin on his face. He took a seat in the emptying terminal lobby and gestured to her to do the same. He handed her what she now recognized as a script. It was titled *Yes And (ish)*.

"Take it from the top," he said softly, but still firmly, as a natural director.

Just as they would have done during any given rehearsal, they proceeded to read the script out loud to each other. They did not have to put on voices or do characters. The script stated they would be playing themselves in this scene.

Yes And (ish):

A pretty girl hesitates to board a plane staring at her through the terminal window. Sitting next to her is a familiar face. One she has laughed with before.

LILLY
What are you doing here?

LEE
I know when we started this whole thing, you had this rule
about not falling in love with you. But it was just too
easy. You have this laugh, that when I heard it for the
first time, I thought to myself, "What the hell was that?"
But you always followed it up with this smile that my words
have always struggled to describe.
However, I am a writer, and it is my job to find those
words. So, here's my attempt:
Your smile.
Your laugh.
Your life.
All of it completely saved mine. Wherever you end up, just
know that I believe in you. And don't ever let fear or life
itself get in the way of your heart. Because that, my
friend, is the most brilliant thing I have ever had the good
fortune of lying next to all those late nights I stayed up
wishing I were someone better.
Someday when this life is nearly over, I'll be thinking to
myself, "You stupid fool, you still have no idea how lucky
you were. You found the most beautiful smile in the world."

She stands up with her bags in hand, still wishing she could
walk away with him, but now realizing it was never in the
cards. He's not here for ever after. Rather, it is for the
perfect goodbye.

LEE
I can't keep you, Lilly. You've got dreams waiting to take
off behind you.

LILLY
What do I do when I think I can't go on?

LEE
Just shut up and laugh.

She smiles at him one last time. They always left each other
laughing. They both know today is the exception. She turns
away from him. She does herself the favor of not looking
back. She knows he loves her too. And that is good enough
for her.

"That's your cue," Lee said, collecting the script back from her.

They hugged. Neither wanted to pull away at first, but he initiated it. When she looked at him, a tear fell to his cheek. She rubbed her thumb across his cheek to wipe away his tear. The final boarding call could now be heard behind her.

After taking two deep breaths like she always took, she smiled at him and said, "Kiss me like you would have tomorrow."

Without hesitation, Lee leaned in and kissed her as perfectly as she could have wished for. He breathed in her exhale and continued to kiss her. After a dozen kisses or so, he stopped. With her eyes still closed, she turned her back to him. As she turned away, she smiled and cried at the same time.

She grabbed her luggage firmly, stood up straight, and began to walk to the entrance of the ramp. Before she was out of sight, she paused. She knew if she turned around, that was it. She was going to stay forever. He knew that too, and was hoping she wouldn't turn around. Once more, she took two deep breaths. She turned her head just enough for him to see her smile one more time. She exited onto the ramp and was out of sight.

When she boarded the plane, of course, she got the window seat facing the terminal window. She dared to look back at it. She could see Lee. He was now wearing the red clown nose she had given him.

Lilly began to chuckle. She then couldn't help but laugh out loud. She looked like a crazy person as she covered her mouth and cried harder and laughed louder. Looking crazy no longer mattered to her.

All that mattered was that someone she loved was smiling back at her.

Both their hearts were racing when the plane left the ground and took off toward the endless sky. With the sun in Lilly's eyes, and the clouds seemingly at her fingertips, it was heaven.

Lee imagined how beautiful she was as the clouds reflected off her eyes. He wondered if she were still guessing what the clouds looked like. A dog? A face? Or perhaps they were just pearly gates opening to an entirely new heaven.

He stood there reliving every memory he had of her. Every set up. Every punchline. Every laugh. Every kiss, whether it was real or dreamt. He could still taste her lips on his own. He could still feel her heartbeat. That one was his favorite.

He knew she loved him too. And that was good enough for him.

That was why he lied to her.

Marilyn Monroe

I f only Lilly had known the truth, she never would have boarded the plane. Lee knew this. He knew she would fall apart and go back to being a trapped soul. Everything would have been for nothing. She didn't deserve that. When Lee had received the call during the film festival, it was to inform him of a terminal cancer diagnosis.

Three months after she had landed, Lilly called him. She was still unaware of the reality of Lee's fading condition. Fortunately, she called him on a good day.

She started with her typical greeting. "Hello, old friend."

"Who is this?" he asked jokingly. "How's the world looking by you?"

"Not bad. The clouds are out and about, but no rain in the forecast today, which is fortunate because I need a new umbrella. The one I have now could not handle another drop. Guess where I'm calling you from?"

"The moon?"

"Ha! Guess again!"

"Well, I look like shit today, so as long as it is not my front door, I'm happy for you."

"I'm calling you from a payphone!" Lilly was so excited to have found one. "These are so rare! It got me all in a vintage mood and thinking about the 90's. I thought about the one person I know who misses those days even more than I do. So yeah. I'm calling you from a payphone. I knew you would appreciate it."

Lee saw right through her rambling conversation and cut to the chase. "What's the scene, Lilly?"

"I'm sorry?" she asked, pretending to be confused.

"What's the scene that you're struggling with?"

"What makes you think I'm calling for acting advice?" she asked with a dismissive chuckle. Lee remained silent on the phone until she relented the truth. She finally did and explained, "I'm auditioning for a play. I'm not sure how to find the character."

"You wouldn't be asking my advice if it were a comedy."

"It's a drama/comedy. It's a series of scenes and monologues told by dead Hollywood celebrities. The part I'm reading for is—"

"Gilda Radner," he guessed, thinking he beat her to the punch.

"Ha! No! That would be easy. The part is Marilyn Monroe. Call me crazy, but I believe I can do it. Physically I can. I have a makeup artist who does amazing work, and we found the perfect wig. But, when it comes to being her, there is something about her that seems to be calling me to this role. I don't know what it is, but I thought you might know." She paused to light up a cigarette she had just bummed from a stranger.

He paused as well to give her inquiry a good, deep thought. He closed his eyes and imagined he was there with her. He let his imagination take him away.

He tapped on the phone booth. He startled her, which made him laugh. She got out of the phone booth and smacked him in the arm playfully as she always did. She looked him up and down. He'd never looked so handsome. While her eyes flirted, she did a double-take once she noticed London Bridge behind him. "There's no payphones on London Bridge."

"It's my fantasy. Just roll with it," he replied as he took the cigarette from her.

He took a long, satisfying drag as they walked along the bridge with Big Ben in the distance. It was time for Lee to put his directing hat on one last time. He began by asking her a simple question. "Why do you want to play her?"

"I know this woman," Lilly said confidently. "She has a face the whole world could draw from memory. Yet, I feel like that's not what she saw in the mirror. Maybe that is why I want to play her. Perhaps, we both had days when our shadows were easier to find than ourselves."

Lee put his arm around her and began his character analysis. "You once told me that great actors wear three masks on stage; the tragic, the comedic, and the one that hides them both. Marilyn appears on the surface like she's not that deep of a person. At a quick glance, we all remember her through overly-filtered red lipstick, wavy blond hair, and a white dress she couldn't keep down. But after a quick glance at her soul, we see a different human being. One that didn't smile too often. One that suffered multiple miscarriages. All she wanted in life was to hold someone else the same way she always dreamed of being held. She could never have that, and therefore, she could never have true happiness. What is life without that?"

Lilly took the cigarette back from Lee and replied, "Empty. Painful. Even more so because she—"

"I," he corrected her. "I, not she or her. Talk in the first person. You are now her thinking out loud."

She took a moment to gather Marilyn's thoughts, and spoke them to Lee. "I have pain. Emptiness. I have to hide that from the camera I'm being paid to smile for. I'm feeling weak—"

"Don't tell me you *feel*," he corrected her again. "I know you *feel*, therefore you *are*. Just as I *am*."

"I *am* weak. Useless. Numb. I am used, but I'm addicted to the need for a strong, protective figure to watch over me, while also wanting to be free and unattached. It's because I am a bird that is addicted to the thrill of taking off." She exhaled her last drag and found Marilyn's smile as she watched the smoke rise high above her head.

Lee took the cigarette back from Lilly. He took one last drag and tossed it into a nearby puddle. He continued on, "Your beauty and your smile are your strength, because they hide the fact you have no strength. No courage. No hope. No ever after."

Lilly got a chill from that and responded, "Why do I get up in the morning?"

He smiled back at her with the words that Jackie once shared with him. "Because you know that love is never ideal, and that happiness is not forever. Therefore, sorrow is not forever either."

She took a moment to contemplate what that really meant. Then came her final thought. As herself. "I know how to play a lonely person. That is not the issue. The issue I have with connecting with her on a higher level is because loneliness was my strength. My happy place. That was where I would dream the most. I dream in the same places people fall apart. That's why I question if I can dig up enough pain. I think for her, it's the pain of being alone reminded her how much she hated life's many ambiguities. But again, I have always cherished ambiguity. I don't know what it's like to suddenly hate it."

Lee thought for a moment and responded perfectly. "Do you know the real reason why I was always in love with you?"

"Why?" she asked, suddenly feeling fragile and dying to hear what he was going to respond with.

He paused for a moment as if he were going to tell her something beautiful. Instead, he hung up the phone.

Now, back in reality, no longer in London, she stood alone in the phone booth. Puzzled. It took her a few seconds to put it all together, but when she realized the meaning of hanging up the phone on her, she could not be more thankful.

He gave her a taste of ambiguity. He then took it away. Swiftly. She now knew what it felt like to hate ambiguity. That was the missing piece.

The next day, she got the part.

Lee returned to his laptop and finally added a title to his finished novel. It was to be called "Ever After."

It was a simple story about a boy who fell in love with a girl who had a particular way of dunking her Oreos in her wine. It was the hopeless romantic story he had always wanted to write.

Filled with ambiguity.

McCarthy Park

In a cancer center in Chicago, Lee sat by himself and received his chemo in silence. The radio would not work. His phone had no signal. The television on the wall had a repair order taped to it. In the corner of the room was a working piano, but no one knew how to play. There was not even one bird singing outside on that sunny day. Lee wondered if this was God's way of telling him to pray. If it was, Lee did admire how much of a wiseass God had learned to be with him.

A nurse who was working her first shift came in to check on Lee. Lee could not place her, but he knew he had seen her before. He saw the name "Lisa" on her nametag, but it did not help his memory. He looked closely at her blue eyes, the flow of her brown hair, and the curve of her dimple as it stretched across her soft face. She casually greeted him and checked to see that he was comfortable. When Lee made a simple joke, she smiled at him, and that was when he was able to place her. When he did, he almost died in his chair.

"Excuse me," he said as he caught the wind that was knocked out of him. "Where did you grow up?"

She answered, "I grew up in Homer Glen. It's a suburb about an hour south of here."

"Did you watch Fourth of July fireworks at McCarthy Park when you were a kid?"

She looked surprised that he would know that. She nodded and replied, "Every year. Of course, that was back in the nineties, which still seems like yesterday to me. Well, you look like you're my age, so you understand. Did you grow up out there?"

"I grew up in Tinley Park. McCarthy was two blocks away from my house. I used to go there every year, too."

Lisa pulled up a chair and sat down next to him. She enjoyed nostalgic conversations and continued to think back. As she smiled back at one particular memory, she added, "I remember every Fourth of July they had a live band on the baseball diamond. My girlfriends and I would always get there early so we could get in a few rounds of miniature golf before the big crowds came. Then we would pig out on cheese fries and scope out the boys coming in." She paused for a moment as one memory came to mind that she appeared to be stuck on.

"What?" he asked, as she smirked for a second and shook her head.

"Nothing. I just…" She just rolled her eyes, and continued, "You know how sometimes you start reminiscing about something, and all of a sudden a random memory just pops out at you?"

He sat up a bit and grinned. "Do tell."

"I remember this one year we all decided to show up to the McCarthy fireworks with dates. My one girlfriend ended up marrying the guy she took there, but the rest of us ditched our dates after the band wrapped up their set." The nostalgia of the lost memory made her laugh and shake her head even more. She had found something within the past that she had not thought about in over twenty years.

As she silently stared back into her memory, he snapped her out of it by jokingly adding, "Don't worry, I wasn't the date you ditched."

She laughed at his joke, but she couldn't take her eyes off that memory. She sank a little deeper into her seat and explained while she chewed on her thumbnail, "Like I say, I just remember the most random things. Like for example, that night we were all standing there watching the

192

fireworks, and I turned my head away for a second to glance around the crowd. I was so busy being jealous of all the happy couples in the crowd, that I almost overlooked this boy right in the middle of it all. He was my age. He looked lost, but not worried about it. He just looked at me and smiled. I smiled back at him. It was as if we knew each other. It was as if we had a whole conversation over a few blinks. His eyes were so kind. Every time I think about that memory, I always wished I would have said something to him."

"What would you have said?" he asked.

"Hi. I'm Lisa." She shrugged, not knowing what else she would have said.

Lee reached out his hand and offered to shake hers. When she shook his hand, confused, he smiled and said to her, "Hi. I'm Lee."

She sat still when he said that. Frozen. Lee knew it was more of a nervous shock than an uncomfortable bombshell. He just continued to politely smile back.

Her inability to grasp the moment caused her to fumble incoherent words into a sloppy laugh. She shook her head and said, "That was smooth. You had me going there for a second. I guess I really walked into that one." Feeling a little jumpy at the silence that followed, she got up and began to exit. "Everything looks good here. Just let me know if you need anything else."

"It was summer '99. You were wearing blue jeans, and a red Abercrombie and Fitch shirt with yellow lettering. You had front bangs, with your hair held back with a white scrunchie. The white didn't match the rest of your attire, but it didn't matter."

She now believed him. "It belonged to my friend. I lost mine at the golf course."

They both stared at each other the same way they had all those years ago. They slowly unraveled years of growing up and could once again see themselves as kids. At least, that was how Lee imagined the moment.

When his eyes glanced over at a nearby mirror, the reflection did not show a dying man and a nurse. Instead, he saw two teenage kids sitting next to each other.

From time to time, growing up, she had thought about what she would have said if she had the chance. The chance was now right next to her. Dying. She knew his prognosis. She couldn't help but address the obvious. "I wish I wasn't meeting you like this…"

"Who cares about that? I don't. Everyone who comes in here asks if I am prepared for the five stages of grief. Truth is, I went through all of them already before I was ever sick. Love walks on the same sidewalk as grief."

"Are you scared?" she asked, hoping it didn't sound like too grim of a question. She held his hand just in case it was.

"I was… until you walked in. Now, that may seem heavy to you, but allow me to explain. See, my whole life I was a writer. We tend to be obsessed with stories that do not have clear endings. We love the good ones. We can live with bad ones. The ones that have no endings…well, fortunately, I only had one of those left. Now, it's like the end of a long movie. You just wait to see if there's anything else after the credits." He paused for a moment to push away any discomfort. He then resumed with his recollected smile, "I can still remember the song the band was playing at that moment. Can you?"

She remembered. She had a look of indecision on her face, but it wasn't toward the song. It was something else.

Finally, she let her own shyness ease up and sat down at the nearby piano. She knew how to play but had always refused to play in front of other people. She always kept her skills a secret. Even to her friends. Today would be her only exception. She placed her fingers on the keys and began to play "I Don't Want to Miss a Thing" by Aerosmith. It was the most beautiful cover Lee had ever heard in his life.

For the rest of his treatments, she would be right by his side. She knew the joy of reminiscing was a painkiller in itself. She was there even on her off days.

On the Fourth of July, even though Lee was beginning to fade, he and Lisa went to McCarthy Park for fireworks. It was the happiest day of his life. He got to be a kid again.

The whole evening was spent reminiscing about the old neighborhoods they grew up in. They both shared stories of long walks to 7-Eleven to get summer slurpies. They both shared what songs they used to stay up waiting for on the radio. They both missed the days of watching *Simpsons* and *Seinfeld* at the dinner table and fearing the *Unsolved Mysteries* theme song. They laughed so hard at how much random useless knowledge they still remembered from MTV's *Pop-up Video.*

It was a different world not too long ago. For both of them, it was still close enough they could touch it. She was a kid again as well. She kissed him as the fireworks concluded.

They too would have fallen in love so easily. Both knew that. And yet, neither lost sleep thinking about how it could have been. They became best friends, and remained that way until the moment Lee closed his eyes for the last time.

The last thing he saw was her face. The kindness in her eyes encouraged him not to be scared, but rather to be free to get up and leave the theater now that the final credits were through.

Acceptance

All Lee had wanted to do near the end was to stay alive long enough to hear about Lilly's opening night from her first performance in London. Opening night was on a Friday. Lee passed away the Monday before.

Lilly was still unaware of Lee's condition. He did everything he could to keep it a secret up until the very end. When the news made its way over to Lilly, she was in the middle of an afternoon rehearsal.

The show was called "Last Call." It was a show about dead celebrities hanging out in a bar in purgatory. The director and Lilly were taking a break to discuss the show. Lilly's director was a sixty-year-old, well-experienced theater director named Elliot Williams. Everyone called him Doctor Williams. He achieved this nickname because in thirty-plus years of directing shows, he never once ran into an issue that he could not fix. His problem-solving intelligence for executing theatrical excellence in the face of uncertainty was legendary. He once turned a twelve-man play into an award-winning solo performance. When an actor quit halfway through a live performance, he grabbed an understudy and altered the premise of the show to include an alternate timeline subplot. He was brilliant. He loved working with Lilly.

While on a break, Lilly and Dr. Williams were discussing the closing scene. Dr. Williams wanted all the characters to exit the bar and head into the unknown light one by one. This would represent the spirits crossing over. He felt Lilly's Marilyn Monroe character should kick the scene off with a short monologue of some kind. He wanted it to be something that gave death both a welcoming charm and a sense of dignity.

They rehearsed idea after idea, but they could not find anything natural that fit the scene. He knew Lilly could find it. The look on her face seemed like she was closing in on an idea. It was at this moment that Lilly was approached by one of her castmates.

The actor walked over to her, put his hand on her shoulder, and said, "Have you read your YouTube comments today?"

"I haven't read them in a while. Why do you ask?" she inquired, while still flipping through her script.

"I was just showing some of the cast a scene from your film, and we started reading the comments. We noticed a bunch of them are from today…" The actor was fine up until this point, but then he could not get the rest of the words out once he knew that she did not know.

Lilly pulled out her phone and began to scroll through the comments. They were all from fans of the documentary that were aware of the news about Lee and were sending condolences to her. At that moment, she was convinced she was dreaming. Whenever she did find herself in a dream, she could always wake up by spotting one significant detail that was out of place. She glanced at the world around her. Everything appeared perfectly in order. She was now terrified knowing that she was awake.

Lilly got up on the stage as if she were walking away from the news that still did not register through the numbness. There was no way it could be true, she thought. If anything, Lee had probably made a comment about graveyards and digging ditches like he always did, and someone misinterpreted his stupid morbid metaphors. That made perfect sense to her. She chuckled at the silliness of it. She felt the urge to call him and make fun of him for it.

"Lilly, I am so sorry," the actor said, not knowing what else to say.

The clueless understudy who had just walked back in from lunch chimed in, "What's with all the weird faces?"

The actor replied to her, "Lilly's friend, Lee, died."

"He's not dead!" Lilly swung around with an even more odd chuckle. She tried to shake off the dozens of sympathetic eyes looking right through her. She tried to chuckle on some more and looked everywhere but their eyes. Even when she looked away, she could feel them. The silence in the theatre began to make her dizzy. Her shaky hand pulled out her cellphone as she again brushed off their looks nonchalantly. "I just need a second. Please. Just need a second here...once I, um, get a hold of...hold on...Watch. He'll pick up his phone. Trust me. Watch...watch...watch..." She began to dial his number. She began to become physically weak when there was no dial tone.

Finally, the automated voice from the other side of the line spoke up, "The number you have dialed is no longer in service. Please hang up or try again."

The silence that followed was when Lilly knew he was gone. Her castmates lowered their heads as they saw the truth sink in on her face. Many tried not to look directly at her. Some could not help themselves.

Lilly tried to dial his number again. When she was met with the automated voice the second time, she collapsed to the ground. She cried harder than she ever had before in her life.

Dr. Williams told everyone to go home for the day. He stayed, but placed himself right outside the entrance to the theatre. One of the actors turned around to go back inside to attend to Lilly.

"No," Dr. Williams gestured him back.

"Sir, she needs a shoulder to cry on," the actor insisted.

Dr. Williams put his hands on the actor's shoulders and said, "Right now, you cannot see it, but there's angels sitting next to her. Comforting her in absolute silence. Trust me, kid. She needs to cry to them first."

Everyone trusted Dr. Williams. This actor was no exception. He walked away as Dr. Williams leaned against the door, making sure no one walked in to disturb Lilly. He glanced at his watch a few times and nodded to himself as her cries got louder. He knew very well the symphony of sorrow. He had lost his daughter at a young age. He felt from his own experience that when souls are rocked to their core with sadness and grief, it was best to get out of the way of the angels.

Dr. Williams stood outside the theatre door for twenty minutes, praying with a rosary he always kept in his pocket. He then took a deep breath, nodded to himself again, and reentered the theater.

Lilly had not moved from her spot. She was curled up in a ball center stage. She was still crying and clutching her chest. Dr. Williams sat down beside her and said nothing at first. He just wanted her to know he was there. He knew the right time to speak up but waited for her to collect herself enough to listen. Ten minutes had gone by. Finally, he spoke up.

"There's nothing I can say that will help right now. We both know that. I need you to understand that I know how you feel right now. I lost my daughter. She was only twenty-two. There are no words. Not for a moment like this." Dr. Williams then lay on his back next to her and continued after a moment of silence, "I know you loved him. Tell me about that. It is going to sting at first, but I promise you, I'm not the only one that is listening."

Lilly did not move at first, but then, she lurched up, still feeling as if she were going to faint, and spoke in a weak voice, "I should have kissed him longer. He met me at the airport while I waited for my flight to come here. I wasn't going to board the plane, but he knew I had to."

"Was he right?"

After a pause that seemed to imply yes, she responded, "I just wish

199

that when he kissed me for the last time, I would have held on. I would have taken my time doing what I always did. I would grab his shirt by his waist, then I would slide my hands up his chest, and then grip my hands softly behind his head. My fingers curling on the back of his neck. I would have held that kiss until the last possible second. But I had a plane to catch. And I had to be the fool who walked away without looking back."

Dr. Williams continued to nod and sit in silence. He had more he wanted to say, but knew it was in Lilly's best interest to be a presence that allowed her mind to speak aloud. He took off his blazer jacket and put it around her as he noticed her goosebumps.

She continued, "I never knew he was sick. I know when we were at the premiere, he told me he went in for a test, and that everything was fine so, how can he..." She looked at her director, who just sat still, letting her mind go to work. She realized everything at that moment. "Did he lie to me? ...He lied to me... Lee wasn't one to lie though. Even when I wished he would... How could I not know he was sick?"

The director exhaled a guilty sigh, and then looked her straight in the eyes. "You were never meant to know anything."

"What do you mean?" Lilly asked in confusion.

"When you were cast for this show, you told your friends from Chicago about it. You also told your friends who was directing it. They told Lee, who looked me up."

Then came a pause.

"That's right. I spoke to him, Lilly." As he shocked her with that truth, he moved on. "He told me, personally, that he did what he had to do to get you over here. And nothing, not even his sickness, was to get in the way of you completing your first opening night in London. When the show run was done, he was going to call you and tell you the truth, but when things took a turn for the worse, he told me one last thing ... whatever happens...no matter how hard she falls...don't put in the

200

understudy."

"You knew he was dying, and you never felt the need to say something to me?"

"No." Dr. Williams continued to look at her with no regrets and said, "Life is short. When you're dying, it is even shorter. So yes, I gave a dying man my word that I would say nothing because the last thing he wanted out of his own life was to see you living yours. I keep my promises."

"Well, fuck you for doing so, doctor. God damnit! Why do you have to think like everyone else!? Everyone thinks they know what's best for me! You don't know what's best for me! You have no right to think you do!" She got up to pace away, but swung around and leaned in. "Tell me I'm wrong!" She got down to his eye level and added, "Look me in the eyes and tell me I'm wrong. You cannot!"

He looked her in the eyes, took a drawn-out pause, and then said, "I do not intend to use the understudy. Having you perform on this stage was Lee's last wish."

"Yeah, well, Lee's dead. Doesn't look like I have worry about breaking his heart now, do I?"

On that note, she walked out. She had no intention of coming back. She hated Lee for breaking her heart, while also not giving her a chance to say goodbye. She felt too many of their moments had unspoken thoughts that should have been told truthfully. She never had the nerve to say she was in love, and never was one to spoil the moment when she felt she was ahead. She hated herself as well.

Before she arrived at her apartment, she first stopped at the local liquor store. She opened a bottle of Patron, took shots, and blacked out thinking about every moment she was a whisper away from saying "I love you" into his ear.

* * *

Lilly woke up the next morning and began a two-day solo bar crawl. She knew it was not the right decision. She did not care. She wanted an anesthetic for the reality she was trapped in. Something where she could physically and mentally be numb and not idle. She looked at it as a smoke break from life.

Whenever a tavern would cut her off, she would walk around to the nearest one that would still serve. Sometimes the walks would be long. She would trip into people, but fortunately for her, they were kind enough to appreciate her look of misery and not escalate her troubles.

* * *

On her second day of drinking, she felt more adventurous and took the London Railway in random directions and drank at several different locations. Her mind was more stimulated by the history of where she traveled, which made her feel better up until she was completely lost. She stopped in a random pub to figure out how to get home. There were no friendly faces.

After listening to Lilly's slurred dilemma, the bartender looked at her with cold eyes. "Up a creek is what you are. Nearest railway isn't running anymore. Gonna be quite the walk home, love. Better figure something out as you sip on last call. Cause I'll tell you one thing, you don't want to be wandering the streets out here."

Lilly felt a panic attack coming. She was a long way from home with no sense of direction, barely enough energy to stand, and a mind that was quickly falling asleep. She did not want to call any cast members, for fear they would spread stories about her to the others. She did not want to call Dr. Williams, but after she dropped her last call on the floor, she did.

It took him a long time to get out to where she was, but when he finally arrived, he saw Lilly shivering outside the closed tavern.

Terrified of every stranger that walked by, she had spent the whole time waiting for him cowering behind a dumpster.

Dr. Williams got out of his car, walked over to Lilly, and spoke to her the same way he wished he could have spoken to his daughter. "It's okay. I'm here now. You're safe. Let me take you home."

For the first few minutes of that long ride home, Lilly said nothing. She just leaned her head up against the cold window and watched her breath fog up the glass. Her eyes began to roll to the back of her head. For a moment she was asleep. She would have passed out, but a speed bump jolted her awake. With that jolt, she felt more coherent. More awake. Soberish.

She sat up in the seat, but continued to look out the window. Dr. Williams said nothing to her. He did not want to be a lecturer. He missed being a father figure but did not let that persuade him to speak first. He waited patiently for her to speak to him.

Finally, turning bleary eyes toward him, she gently asked, "When your daughter died…how long did it take before you could blink without it hurting?"

Mr. Williams thought about his answer. Where to begin? So much to say. "My daughter and I never got along. She wasn't exactly daddy's little girl. She loved her mom, and her mom hated me. What can you do? We fought a lot. Always saying things to each other that we both pretended not to regret." He stopped his story when he saw her eyes were closed.

"I'm listening," she said with her eyes still closed.

He continued, "At twenty-two, she came to me and said she had a brain tumor. We sat on my porch that day and talked for hours. She was different that day. She was so sweet. Forgiving. When I asked if she was scared, she told me the moment she knew the end was approaching, something wonderful happened within the sadness. She was incapable of feeling fear. She couldn't feel regret or anger anymore. It was as

203

if it just magically went away. All she could feel was the humility of seconds going by. Every breath remaining had the same feeling as you feel when you cry laughing. She wished I could feel as she felt. Not a worry in the world. Just love." He took a pause and pulled out a photo of them from that day. They looked so happy. "I carry that around with me wherever I go. Because it is a reminder of what she told me that day. She told me to not hold on to disappointment, or fear, or anger. Because only love comes with."

The rest of the car ride was mostly quiet. When they pulled up to her apartment, Mr. Williams handed her a small package that was addressed to her.

"This arrived at the theatre today. It's addressed to you, but they wrote down the theatre address. It's from Frank and Jackie."

"Thanks. I'll open it up tomorrow." Lilly gave the doctor a hug and went on her way. She turned around as she passed the driver side door and said, "Your daughter was beautiful. I'm glad you guys got to have that day."

"She's with me every day. Just because I won't see her tomorrow, doesn't mean she's not there."

She nodded and took in those words. They did resonate as she flashed back to when a clown once told her how some things aren't meant to last, but still manage to find forever.

"You want to come watch the show tomorrow? I think I figured out what the understudy will say at the end."

Lilly just shrugged her shoulders and waved goodnight. When she went inside her apartment, she tossed the package on the counter and fell asleep on her bed.

* * *

Lilly woke up Friday afternoon without the slightest hint of a hangover.

She slept for twelve hours and had not felt this well rested in a long time. When she got up, she grabbed herself a cup of coffee from her kitchen and made it to go. It was beautiful day in London. Not a cloud in the sky. She walked around and kept thinking over what Dr. Williams had told her. Only love comes with.

She began to get this crazy thought in her head. She did not know how spirits worked, or how the afterlife functioned, but what if Lee was still around? What if there was a God? If there was, what if he knew Lee's scheme, and granted him another day on Earth to see Lilly perform? What if God was that kind to Lee, but she wasn't on the stage? Her imagination went in several different directions, but it kept leading her back to the same thought. What if Lee came to see the show, but she was in the audience cheering on the understudy? He would be so pissed, she thought. That thought made her laugh, and it was her first laugh in five days.

While walking around and playing with spiritual ideas in her head, she found a quiet bench near a pond where only the breeze seemed to speak. It was peaceful and calm. No clouds to block out the sun, which was perfectly fine. She felt she could use some warmth. She finished her coffee and opened Frank and Jackie's package.

Once unwrapped, she saw a sympathy card and what looked like a small jewelry box. The card said if she needed anything, Frank and Jackie would be on the next flight to London. The card concluded by stating that inside the box was something Lee left for Lilly.

Lilly held the box in her hands and took a few deep breaths. She did not know if she was ready for this, but knew the warm sun would quickly dry what tears might come.

She opened it.

Inside was her original red clown nose. It was the one that was given to her as a child. The same one she had given to Lee. He was now passing it back to her. Along with it was a handwritten note from Lee:

Shut up and laugh.

Oh, and take this with you.

Because it's magic.

A few hours later, Lilly showed up to the theatre and knocked on Dr. Williams's door. When he opened it, she looked him in the eye with the cockiest grin and said, "I'm ready."

Dr. Williams nodded, but then shook his head and said, "I wish you had your epiphany sooner. I already told the understudy she could go on tonight."

Lilly was not sure what to do next. Neither was Dr. Williams. At that moment, the understudy walked in, right behind Lilly, holding the Marilyn Monroe wig. Lilly could tell she wanted to be out on the stage so badly.

The understudy looked at Dr. Williams. She then looked at Lilly. With a sudden smirk on her face, she said, "That damn wig don't fit." She tossed the wig to Lilly and smiled. "Go get 'em."

* * *

The show opened to a sold-out audience. Everyone was nervous, and it showed. The first two scenes were hard to watch as actors struggled with their timing. The audience grew timid and felt on edge, hoping the actors could get through the scene without another whisper of one actor giving another actor their missing line. The atmosphere was heavy. Nothing was in sync. And then it was time for Lilly to take the stage in her first appearance as Marilyn Monroe.

In this scene, Marilyn came out and greeted everyone as the owner of the bar in purgatory. From the moment she stepped onto the stage, her eyes took charge of the room. They gently pushed the audience back into their seats to relax, while at the same time pulling their ears closer to listen to her hilarious improvisations. Within minutes, she held the audience in her hand while her heartbeat tried to keep up. When her first scene was finished, the audience applauded as the stage lights faded to a blackout.

Her second appearance was two scenes later. In this scene she got to referee a drinking contest between Elvis and James Dean. It was by far the most hilarious scene of the show. Then came the moment that made Dr. Williams the most anxious. The final scene.

Marilyn was to quit her job as manager of the bar to go find out how to cross over to her final destination. Though Dr. Williams and she had brainstormed what to say at this moment, they never solidified it. Dr. Williams was sweating in his seat, as this scene was crucial to the finale. What would she say, and would her improvisation hit home enough for the audience to appreciate the theme of leaving what you've always known to find what you've always been meant for?

Marilyn sat on the edge of the stage carrying four shots. She handed one to an audience member and saluted him. "Cheers. I have no idea who you are, but that doesn't mean I wasn't thankful that you came along." They took the shot together and she hugged him. She then took the other two shots and handed one to a female audience member. They raised their glasses and Marilyn said, "Cheers…I don't know who you are…but I slept with your husband many times. No. I'm just kidding." The audience laughed while they took their shots. Marilyn hugged this audience member as well and said, "I don't know who you are, but I hope you find happiness and joy like an imaginative child on an endless playground." Marilyn then sat back on the edge of the stage and looked out over the audience with a calm glance. She put her shot glass upside down beside her and smiled at the audience, perfectly in character. She was sexy, but graceful, as she continued, "Sometimes, in this life, you choose to stay longer than you were invited for. How can you not? Life is unpredictable. No one is exempt. But, what we fear, what we hate, what makes us broken, we do not take with us. Only love comes with." She smiled at her audience as they seemed to take in what she was saying. "Don't cry when it's time to leave. Don't try to cheat time. You can't. Sometimes, all you can do is just wait your turn to cut in and dance. Then, you just rest your head against something beautiful. Until the last note." Marilyn now stood center stage and somehow managed to look everyone in the eye at once. "Only love comes with. That's how I know you and I will always be alright. Because even if we don't see tomorrow together, that doesn't mean you won't be with me." With that, she headed toward the stage exit, but first she put a dollar in the piano man's tip jar. She whispered a request in his ear. He began to play *La Vie En Rose*. On that cue, she gave everyone a final look back. She smiled and headed into the light of the exit. "See you when I see you."

The piano player played on as the other characters made their exit one by one until the lights completely faded to black. The response from the audience was an immediate standing ovation. When Lilly came out to take her bow, she saw tears rolling down Dr. Williams's face. He walked down the main aisle as roses were being tossed on the stage, and handed one personally to Lilly. As she took it, she hopped off the stage to give him the biggest hug.

Both had voids in their heart that they had helped each other to fill. Lilly's soul could once again breathe.

* * *

When she came back to Chicago, she found the cemetery where Lee was buried and paid him a visit on a beautiful autumn day.

As she was entering, she nodded to Lee's teacher, Ms. Murphy, who was leaving. Back at her apartment, Ms. Murphy had a picture of Lee on her mantel, which helped to hold up the enormous Fighting Irish flag he had given her as a thank you for filling seats for Lilly's show.

Back at the cemetery, Lilly found Lee's grave and sat next to it. She grinned playfully. "Well played, asshole."

She pulled out a sealed letter, the words inside to be known only between herself and Lee. In the most sentimental words that would have impressed the writer himself, she explained how his soul would always have a home with hers. She now believed that the soul's journey did not end at death, but rather began again as the eyes closed and the stars from the universe above called upon the soul to find its place among the stars.

She laid the letter on his grave, believing to herself that he could not wait to read it.

She then pulled out the red rubber nose, placed it firmly above her smile, and rested in the grass next to him. She would never tell a soul the full extent of what her heart confessed in that letter. All she would tell people was how it ended:

P.S. The birds are singing today.

The End

About the Author

Paul Teresi attended Eastern Illinois University to pursue a degree in teaching history. He left to pursue a career in writing after creating an independently produced sold out show on his campus. Since then, he has written several stage productions at Chicago's famed Second City Training Center. While performing live shows was his favorite thrill, he has found a new niche in writing his stage stories long hand for publication. His first book *Yes And (ish)* is the first of what he hopes will be many fun comedies brought to life from previous stage productions.

Made in the USA
Columbia, SC
18 July 2021

41971619R00124